Making

Grade

When Almost Nothing Goes Your Way

Naiya Krom

Dear Reader,

This story was written while I was in 7th grade. I am currently a freshman in high school. Soon, Making the Best of 8th Grade will also be available. Thank you to my friends who inspired me and helped me reach my goal - Rachel, Abby, Sara, Reese, Haley, and all my lunchtime friends. I also want to thank my parents and my brother, Canyon, for their love and support. Enjoy!

Naiya

Thank you to everyone who gave me the information and experiences in this book...you know who you are.

September

Chapter 1

Twas the Night Before 7th Grade

Hi! My name is Olivia and I am starting 7th grade tomorrow. Yep! The big 7th grade, which basically just means bigger classes, more teachers, and I'm one of the oldest in my middle school! I am *super* excited! This is going to be my best year yet! Most of my friends- Ella Anderson, Crystal Jace, Katie Smith, Chloe Marielen, Ava Larr and Makayla Hanson- are in my group of classes, which Wood River Middle School cleverly calls "teams". That basically means I get to have classes with them, eat lunch with them, and do gym and my Unified Art's with them. It's seriously awesome.

I should probably tell you a bit about myself before I continue this story. My name is Olivia Kiara Hamilton, and I am 12 years, two months, and twenty nine days old. My birthday is June 9th, and I have a chiweenie named Peanut. A chiweenie is an adorable mix of a chihuahua and a dachshund. In addition, I have long, wavy brown hair, brown eyes and I wear braces. My best friend of all of the people previously mentioned is Ella. And, I couldn't be more excited about starting 7th grade!

I'm setting out my outfit, convincing myself that it doesn't look to babyish for a recently turned 12 year old girl. I'm also dancing around my room, listening to music. I'm pretty sure my friends don't know that I'm doing this right now, and I'm not sure I want them to.

Suddenly my phone-which is most definitely not a smartphone, no matter how many times I beg my parents-beeps. It's a text from Crystal. Crystal and I are really good friends. We started hanging out a few years ago. We text a lot.

Ready for tomorrow?

I smile at my phone as I text back:

Yeah, picking out my outfit now.

She doesn't respond. She's probably getting her outfit ready too. I'm pretty sure she's just as excited as I am for tomorrow. Though, considering I've been looking forward to this since 5th grade, I may be just a little bit more excited than she is, not that it's a competition or anything. It's so exciting because we're the second oldest in the school, and besides, this is an amazing time in our lives. Also, we get to do some new clubs and I we have the privilege of going to school dances.

Anyway, for my outfit, I finally decide on a rainbow shirt with a white sparkly peace sign on it and black pants. Relieved to have that out of the way, I sit on my bed and think about our arrangements for tomorrow. I say "our" because there is a group of us. Ella, Makayla and I planned ahead of time that we'd sit at one of the coveted round lunch tables with some people, whom I call my lunchtime friends, from last year. We had all gotten into the foreign language program and chosen French, so we hoped to be in the same class. With those two things planned out, 7th grade seems a lot less scary and lot more exciting and fun! I get up and go back to dancing. There is way too much energy in me to just sit and do nothing.

"Olivia, mom and dad say to get ready for bed," my 9 year old brother George says. He looks up from his music player at me, raising his eyebrows. "Are you okay?" he asks me.

I nod and smile. He just walks away, shaking his head. In case you are wondering, I'm not really a good dancer, at least not according to my soon to be fourth grade brother. I know, I know, you're shocked.

My stomach does a flip inside as I look at the clock. It's 8:37 p.m.. In less than 12 hours, I will be in school. I get on my pajamas, brush my teeth, wash my face and then rush into my bed. I want to get to sleep as soon as possible. I can't wait!

☮ ☮ ☮

Finally, the morning is here. While posing for pictures my mother insists on taking, my stomach flips inside again. The bus will be here in 20 minutes. In twenty minutes, I will be the second oldest person in the entire middle school. I don't know why my mom makes George get up. His school starts an hour later than mine. But this is his last year of elementary school, which is awesome, because next year I'll have him the the middle school with me. For one year at least, then I'm off to high school. I don't want to think about that. I'm not ready yet. I just turned 12!

When I finally board the bus, I think about the clubs I want to join such as SADD, Student Council, and Yearbook (I get lost in my own thoughts a lot) when suddenly I am tapped on the shoulder. I turn around to see Sierra, an 11 year old who lives a street away from me. I hadn't seen her all summer! She goes to camp so she's not around much.

We talk about how excited we are and she agrees to sit on the bus with me in the afternoon. It's not even 7:15 a.m. and already I found someone who is excited to be around me. Even though I know things never work out the way I want them to when it comes to this sort of thing, I couldn't be happier right now! I feel like the whole day is going my way until the second I step into the yellow hallway. Ella and I are walking, talking, and laughing when we see a sign on the door. Since this list is in alphabetical order, I see Ella's name first.

Ella Anderson, Y2

I get my hopes up for being in Y2 as well. Ella and I do almost everything together, including classes. I look further down the list and find my name, finally.

Olivia Hamilton, Y8

What? I see Makayla walk up behind us. "Oh, Y2! Hey Ella, you're with me! Sorry, Olivia. I'm sure someone is in your class." Makayla smirks at me. Huh? What the heck is that creepy smirk about? She and Ella walk away, and I stand there, trying not to cry. Trying not to cry on the first day of 7th grade. Well, now isn't this nice?

I'm seriously hating 7th grade right now and I've only been here, for, oh, 30 seconds. Great way to start off the school year.

No, I can't let this get in my way. This is supposed to be the best year of my life. If I want that to happen, nothing can ruin it.

Luckily, some friendly faces, Lexi and Lisa, come up behind me. They are in Y8 too, so we walk in there together. I'm glad I finally get to see Lexi, because she's busy a lot. She is definitely the most athletic girl I know and is super nice. Lisa is talkative sometimes, and she is usually fairly quiet but very smart. I met her in 2nd grade when she moved here from Warwick.

I'm not even in Y8 for 5 minutes when we listen to announcements. When they end, my teacher, Mr. Lion, starts talking. He says he'll be our math teacher and proceeds to give us orange pieces of paper that are our schedules. I'm glad to see I have math after French. At the end of the day I have English Language Arts (ELA) which has always been my favorite subject.

OH NO! Mr. Lion assigns seats! No. No no no no no no. You may think I'm overreacting, but this is where things always go wrong for me, and I see no reason why they should go wrong now. Because I'm a good student, I get put with the worst kids who never do any work and it annoys me so much. The teachers think I'm going to rub off on them or whatever. News flash: I'm not.

As he assigns seats, I realize that my thinking was correct. I'm the only girl in a group of three of the most trouble making boys in school. Please tell me this isn't happening! AHHHHHHHHHHHHHHHHHH! (This is not a good scream.)

I suffer through math class the best I can with the boys around me talking to each other and I want to slap every single one of them in the face when they ask me if I can stop reading because I'm getting in the way of their game of "Catch the Paper".

Guess what? Catch the Paper is not a game!

I am excited, however, when I walk into French and see Ella, Katie, and another nice girl, Chloe sitting at a table. I rush over, but Makayla shoots me a dirty look and sits down. OK, that was rude. Luckily, my friend Jennifer is in that class, and she waves me over. Grateful for getting the wave, I sit down. "Thanks, Jenny." Seriously, I can't believe my other friends though.

Jenny shrugs referring to the situation. Over the class period, I can't help looking over at Makayla, Ella, Katie, and Chloe. That was supposed to be my seat. I was supposed to be sitting next to Ella, Katie and Chloe and laughing at something no one else would understand. That was supposed to be me in general, not just my seat, my *life*. Ok, I guess that's kind of taking this whole misunderstanding-at least I hope it's a misunderstanding-a little bit too far. I mean, it's just one class, right? I can deal with not sitting next to my best friend in *one class*. Can't I? That's not going to define my life, hopefully.

But, no, I realize it's not just one class. That's how the rest of the day continues. Makayla takes all of the seats and I sit with a different friend in each class. Well, friend is putting it loosely. I sit with an acquaintance, someone whom I have known since kindergarten and never talk to or someone who has probably called me a dork at one time of my school career or another. My favorite class quickly becomes ELA, and I am "glad" to see at the end of the day that I have NO ONE in that class. The only reason I like it is because I really like reading and writing. Still though, I could have at least one friend since everyone else in the class does!

Mrs. Keller assigns seats as soon as everyone is in the classroom, probably so she can learn our names more quickly. She is going to be our teacher for two years. It's probably good that she learns everyone's name now. I breathe a sigh of partial relief as soon as she points out my desk, which is luckily right near the front where I like being. Okay, I can deal with this group. My group consists of Holly, Theo, and Mimi, who I've never hated but never loved either. I mean, it's not like I was looking forward to having any specific person in my group, considering that I don't have any friends in this class so far. At least I'm not the only girl. However, I don't enjoy ELA class as Holly and Mimi talk to each other (since when are *they* lifelong friends?) and don't let me join in with them. When the bell finally rings, I rush out of the room. I'm glad that it's over, finally. I can't help but be a little disappointed with the way the day ended up being like. In my head, it was much different.

I don't think 7th grade is bad, but at this point, I don't think it's great either. Maybe I can be a whole new Olivia in 7th grade. I like that idea. I've always been a bookworm (at least that's how people see me) so maybe this year I can be even a little bit popular. Maybe...possibly...okay, that's never going to happen unless I stop being me entirely. It's still something I can try for but that doesn't mean I'm going to stop being myself to impress others.

Most of the time, I love being who I am and nothing that people will ever do is going to change that about me, no matter how insecure I feel sometimes. I'm unique and I have my friends, but maybe being popular can be my goal. Just because I'm going to keep being myself doesn't mean that I can't try some new things. People can change what they like or do, but they don't change who they are.

That's it! I'm convinced that this is a good idea. This year, I'm changing myself. I will have a positive attitude! I smile the whole way home.

Chapter 2
My Personal Opinion on Gym

I don't like physical education or what we kids call gym and I never have. Sure, in elementary school I may not have hated it, but oh my gosh do I hate it now. The difference is this: in elementary school, all of the grade had gym together, so I was always able to talk to Ella if I wanted. I thought it was going to be the same way in middle school, but I was wrong. Everything changed in 5th grade. In fact, last year I had no friends in my gym class so naturally I talked to the teacher. People *groaned* when they had to partner up with me. I mean come on guys, no one wants to hear that, not even me. And, I'm the kid who everyone except my friends call dorky, who should be used to it by now. I don't like walking down the hallway to enter the gym. I don't like being in the locker room and changing while hoping and praying that no one opens up my curtain. It's happened to other people and I cannot imagine anything worse. I don't like walking around in gym and knowing I'll have to separate from my friends. So... I don't need people to groan when I partner up with them.

I'm going to face the facts. I can't do a decent sit up or push-up, which I'm not proud of, but it's still true. It's still a reason (probably the main reason) why I do really badly in gym. All my friends have fairly good upper body strength. I just don't I guess. I wasn't blessed with that. I was told my academic strength is going to help me later in my life, mostly by my parents. I'm not exactly seeing that now.

Plus, I don't have any friends in my gym class now either, unlike I did in elementary school. Of course Crystal, Ella, Makayla, Chloe, Lisa, Lexi, and Jenny are in a different class which meets at the same time. They all get together. I am alone. But it didn't help that I just got off crutches for spraining my ankle in July. It's like no one knows how much it hurt. Too bad it had to happen in July so I didn't even miss one day of gym. Depressing, I tell you, depressing. Seriously. These are my weeks so far.

Week One

Volleyball. Need I say more? They are assigning teams. Oh, there is one team I don't want. Please don't let me get that team. I just want that other team, the team that all my friends have gotten on so far, not the one with

Holly, Theo, Mimi and James. Please put me on the team that Ava just got on. Oh, please?

I am on the other team - not the one with Ava or my other friends. I feel my face turn red as they laugh at my serve and the hit that I missed. Nothing is going my way today but I try not to mope around. No one is giving me the ball. Just because I'm not good doesn't mean I don't want to try and play. This hour (which seems like an eternity) of gym is a long time to lose hope that people like the way you play volleyball. The ball is coming towards me. I got it! I got it! I can totally hit this. I am going to succeed and surprise the entire the world (aka gym class).

I miss it. Of course I miss it. I couldn't have surprised the world by succeeding. I have to miss and fail. Hope the universe is having fun with itself. Can you guess what happened? Long story short, the doctor doesn't think my nose is broken. She is glad that the nurse called my mom to take me to get it checked.

Week 2

We are playing basketball. I'm usually pretty good at it, so I am fairly confident. They let us pick our teams for this unit. I run over to Makayla and Ella immediately, but Makayla shakes her head at me. Ella shrugs and joins some boys. Since when does Ella, the girl I've known since I was 4, like boys? I don't even like a boy yet. We used to be just like each other, and now, what the heck? I hear them snicker and they look over at me, even Ella. I'm not sure if they are talking about me, but it seems like they are.

Tears form in my eyes, but I don't cry. I turn around. Crystal is on a team with Chloe, Lisa, a girl named Jessica and Jenny, and she lets me in. I think she understands. Her old best friend, Lizzy dumped her in 5th grade. I think she thinks that is what is happening to me.

It's not. Ella and I are fine. We are just at a temporary friendship rough spot right now. At least I like the people on this team. It could be worse, I guess.

I don't score any baskets, but I catch a rebound. No one is happy when I score for the other team. But come on, a basket is a basket!

The teachers are all telling me to concentrate. Yeah, um, okay. So, my best friend is dumping me for someone who started being mean to me and I don't even know why. I already hate gym, and here I am, with people who don't know the real me at all. But yeah, I'll try and focus my attention back on *basketball*. That's my new first priority.

Week 3

Track? After a sprained ankle? I don't *think* so. We have to do the mile run. I'm already not the fastest runner, but I am thrilled when I beat my best time of 15 minutes and 32 seconds. My time for today is 13 minutes and 19 seconds. When my gym teacher hands back our papers, I see, in red pen, 70. What? THAT'S MY BEST TIME! It's not supposed to be a 70. Maybe an 80, it's not an amazing time but it's definitely not a 70! Not even close!

Makayla sees me on the way back to the locker room. "Great job, Olivia," she laughs, "My time was 9:31." I roll my eyes. I am tired of Makayla. She always has to one-up me. She's not even that fast of a runner. I decide to point this out to her, when I realize she's already gone and I look like the weak one. I sigh, hating every little thing about gym class. I don't see Ella, but I'm not sure I want to. She's an amazing runner so I'm sure she'll have a fantastic time.

Now do you understand why I hate gym? Almost everything bad that has ever happened in school has happened in the gym. All those scholar athletes make the non-scholars or the uncoordinated weirdo pants like me feel bad about themselves. I really, really, really, *really* hate gym class.

Chapter 3
After School Activities (finally)

After school activities start the second week of school. I want to do a lot of things, and I try super hard to get into student council. I run for the position of class senator. I know it is a long shot but I will give it a try. I am out the day that everyone gave speeches which turned out to be a positive thing. The class voted for me. I actually won!!!! Maybe I was just underestimating everything. Maybe I am popular! Ok, that's not the case. Maybe they think I'd be a good candidate since I'm not stupid. Yeah, that's probably it. I am super excited as I stay after on Monday.

Things are looking up.

I'm gonna be in student council! I've wanted this since 5th grade! Whoo! Happy dance! Yes, I still need to work on my popularity problem but at least I'm semi-improving little teeny bit by little teeny bit. Still improving! Whoo!

Lexi is at the Student Council meeting on Monday so I sit beside her. "Hi Olivia. Aren't you excited? I've wanted to do this since, like, 5th grade."

I nod. Student council would be great. I may even be Vice President, just like I wanted. The possibilities are endless. Suddenly, the advisor comes into the room. Everyone stops talking and pays attention as she shows a slide show presentation. I leave that day, determined to win that VP spot.

Katie is standing outside the door, cleaning out her locker. I tap her on the back. She turns around. "Hey Olivia. How was student council?"

"Amazing! Why are you cleaning out your locker?" I ask. Katie always has an extremely clean locker, plus, we've only been in school for two weeks. I give her a puzzled look. She smiles up at me and rolls her eyes.

"My locker started out dirty if you can believe it. But I wasn't allowed to stay after and clean it until today. Seriously, look at this!" She shows me an old test paper from someone named Bailey Orday and it had a big, red 29 on the top. I wince and she nods. I decide not to bring up the fact that my locker's already dirty because I am probably the most unorganized person on the planet.

"Ugh, that must be a pain." I remark. She gives me a look that says, "Duh. Obviously." I wave goodbye and leave. My mom is waiting out in the car.

"Hey Olivia. How was school?"

I shrug. "Student council was okay. In history I finished my work and was allowed to read for about 20 minutes. I missed two baskets in gym and Ella wasn't here today." I pretend to pout. Really though, the day wasn't that bad. Not as bad as some of the other days. Not as bad as the first day of school for example.

"Aw. Well, I have a surprise that I think will make today better."

"What?" I question. I am generally confused. Surprises can mean anything. We could be moving for all I know. Or I could be graduating high school now and not have to deal with 7th grade. I already know 7th grade won't be as great as I thought it would be.

"If you are going to be doing all these after school activities, you should have this." My mom pulls out a smart phone.

Wait...what?

A SMART PHONE! OH MY GOSH! I have wanted this since forever. I smile and hug my mom while ready to explode with happiness. George pops up behind the seat and scowls at me.

"Mom? How come Olivia gets a smart phone, but I don't? I'm in 4th grade now." he says, crossing his arms. I roll my eyes. George always wants whatever I want. Finally, being older might actually be good for something other than just being older. Which, believe me, sometimes seems like it's good for nothing.

"George, you already have a perfectly good music player, and Olivia needs this because she stays after school." My mom reasons gently but firmly. George rolls his eyes and makes a face. He is obviously super jealous.

The next day, I tell Crystal about my new phone. I know she's going to be really happy for me. I know she's going say something like, "You've finally joined the real world. Congratulations Olivia." That would be just to tease me, but I won't care. I'd just be happy and she'd be happy for me too. Usually I would tell Ella, but I feel like she wouldn't be happy for me. Crystal on the other hand, gets out her phone and we exchange numbers. I mean, I had her number, but when I got a new phone, I lost it. You get me right?

Yeah, you get me. You're now my best friend in the entire world for understanding me. Thank you, I'll get back to the story now.

TMGD also starts that day so Crystal and I both go to the meeting. It stands for Teens Making Good Decisions. It's kind of cool to be part of this club. We both sit at a seat near the back of the room and listen to the advisor. She talks about what we will be doing this year. We will be doing some projects for our school. We may even be in the Wood River Column, our town's newspaper. I smiled wider when I heard that since I would love to be in the newspaper. What 12 year old girl doesn't?

I was only in it once when I was two. I was sitting in a kayak while shopping at The Outdoor Store with my dad, and a photographer saw it, thought I was cute, and put me in. But that was 10 years ago, of course I want to be in the newspaper again at age 12! And there is no way that I'm going to be getting in for being cute anymore.

Anyway, TMGD is different than Student Council. We are definitely more part of a team than independant. Plus, I have Crystal at the meetings who sits next to me.

Chapter 4
My First Dance

I have been looking forward to my first dance since 5th grade. I had seen all the movies and TV shows where they are magical and romantic. Honestly, nothing seems much better. That's why when the announcement comes on, I smile as big as I can. I can't wait! This is going to be the best day ever!!!!!!!!!!!! I'm almost positive that nothing can ruin this. I've been looking forward to it for way too long. Eventually, I'll find a date to go with. Not this time of course. I don't even like any boys yet. I hope I never will. That would be so stressful, and honestly, I know that I would constantly make a fool out of myself in front of him.

I buy a ticket on the Wednesday before the dance. On that Friday, I come down the stairs from my bedroom wearing my new outfit and my favorite necklace. Crystal will be here any minute. Ella wasn't going to the dance because she really wasn't feeling great today and wanted to rest at home. I understood. Crystal rings the doorbell. I forget everything I was thinking about. Will anyone dance with me? Will I see any of my other friends? Will I see any teachers I knew? Will any of the teachers try to be really cool and dance but instead accidentally humiliate us when our friends from the other team realize that's the person that's giving us our education? Will my friend from the other team, Fiona, start questioning my education? Ok, it's a school dance. I'm thinking way too much into this. I answer the door, but not without my dog, Peanut, barking wildly.

"Sorry Crystal." I have to hold his collar and lean down to keep him from running out the front door after Crystal's mom and their car.

"It's ok, Olivia. Peanut is so cute as always." Crystal pets Peanut right behind his ear, right where he likes it. I'm not sure how she knows it. This is the first time Crystal has ever been over my house. She's so great with animals that she seems to know where he likes to be pet. I guess I'd call it a special talent of hers.

I gave her a smile as my mom comes down the stairs. George follows behind her but is silent. I have to imagine my mom asked him not to embarrass me because he's never just silent.

"Oh Olivia, Crystal, you two look so beautiful. Here, let me take a quick picture and then you guys can go on your way. I can't believe you are going to your first dance." She takes more pictures than she said (she takes like 80) and we get in Crystal's car.

It's a minivan, so there's enough space for the both of us to fit comfortably. The ride there is basically filled with talking about the excitement and small amounts of fear for tonight. Crystal is concerned about getting asked to dance by the guy she likes. I'm not concerned about too much. I mostly just want to have a good time. I mean, it's my first dance. I don't need to dance with anyone yet. I'm only 12. No need for boy drama quite yet, you know? I'm happy that I'm going with Crystal, who I know will make me feel welcome with her more popular friends.

At the dance, Crystal and I stand awkwardly outside the school. We're not speaking. Come on Olivia, say something. Break the ice. Anything would be better than just standing here staring at each other like this. But what am I supposed to say? We talked the entire way to the school, I think we've said what we needed to say in those 5 minutes. Suddenly, Terri and Lexi rush over. Terri is a girl that Lexi has started hanging out with. She met them in 6th grade, last year. I say hi to both of them (mostly Lexi because I don't really know Terri very well) and finally the doors open. We all rush in. It's a mad rush to hand in our tickets and then actually get into the dance. Whew. Thank gosh that's over. I feel like I got through something tough, considering that everyone is being told to stand in a single file line. We just got through. I'm strong, I tell myself. Don't mess with me!

The gym isn't decorated and the lights are on, so frankly, I am kind of disappointed. This looks nothing like it does in the movies. Crystal seems excited though, and it's contagious. Soon I am laughing and smiling too. There are a few eighth graders there, but even that doesn't really make me too nervous. I am excited to just hang out with my friends for a few hours.

The girls mostly hang on one side of the room with the boys on the other for the first 10 or 15 minutes, but when the lights go down, everyone joins together having a great time. Crystal and I start talking and dancing. Soon Makayla comes over. I run over to join her and she gives me a happy smile.

Makayla looks beautiful. She puts a lot more work into her look than I do. She puts on some makeup as well. Today, her dark brown hair is curled slightly and she is wearing a green shirt with a jean skirt and pink flats. She has braces just like I do. She must have just gone to the orthodontist, because her brackets have changed from pink and light orange to blue and yellow.

Crystal, Makayla and I hang out together for most of the night. Not many boys and girls dance together, we mostly just hang out in one big group. During the slow songs most 7th graders go and get a snack or a water bottle. All in all, it's a pretty good night. At 8:30, the dance is finally over and I meet Crystal's mom outside. Suddenly, I realize my necklace charm is missing. Where did it go? Oh, come on. I was having such a good night until this happened to me of all people. Crystal helps me search through the gym which I truly appreciated. She's such a great friend for helping me. It's clear sea glass. How can I ever find that kind of necklace? It's like, impossible. I feel like crying. I had convinced my parents to let me wear that necklace. How do you lose a charm off a necklace? I didn't even know that was even remotely possible. Well, I guess it is, because it happened to me.

When Crystal finally drops me back at home, I spill to my parents what happened. They are very understanding, lucky for me, and tell me to look in the lost and found. I am so thankful to have parents like them. Ugh. So much for a great first dance.

Chapter 5
School Update

So now that it's almost October, most of our classes have started getting harder. The teachers have stopped going easy on us, and are giving us tons of work. Luckily, I haven't had homework on the weekends. I always look forward to Student Council and TMGD. I am still not entirely sure why yearbook hasn't started yet. Last year, it had started about two weeks into the year. Maybe whoever is doing it now is just waiting until later.

October

Chapter 1
Student Council

At the October Student Council meeting, the positions are officially announced. I get excited. I can't wait to start on my campaign! I can do posters and a video, and maybe my friends can be in it, but only if they want to of course. I've stopped paying attention to the advisor as I'm just thinking about student council. I don't want to force anyone to do anything that they don't want to do. Anyway, this is all running through my head when Ella texts me after school:

Olivia, Lexi says u r running for VP in SC
Yep
Makayla wants 2 know if she can b ur campaign manager
I guess so. no 1 else is doing it
Hey, u doing a video

Yeah
Can I b in it
sure
Ok, bye
Bye Els

I feel great. I have a campaign manager, a supportive friend, and a video participant. So when I go to school the next day, I have a huge smile on. I don't have gym either which makes it like 200 times better. You already know my feelings on gym. I feel like I'm walking on a cloud and that cloud is a rainbow. It is a sparkly rainbow which lets you float and fly or sleep or watch TV or write or read or do whatever you want to do. It's amazing trust me. I mean, you probably don't know how I feel right now, so just imagine the best happiness ever times 10.

"Crystal! I am doing a video to be Vice President. Do you want to be in it?" I ask my friend hopefully. Crystal smiles widely and nods in reply. Two video participants! I get so excited! OK, maybe more excited than I should get, but still, tell me this isn't good news. I thought no one would want to help me with this.

The day just keeps getting better and better. Brianna, my best friend from my chorus class, asks if she can be in my video too. I nod and we start singing. After class, she asks when to come over. I tell her the date my mom agreed to, and she gives me a thumbs up as she goes to her own hallway. I just start smiling, leaving people to give me weird looks, but I don't really care. I'M MAKING A VIDEO! I could potentially win this thing. I could be Vice President. It takes all my willpower not to start jumping up and down like a complete psycho.

The day of the video finally comes. When my friends arrive, we start immediately. I have to reject a few ideas because of time available (it has to be under a minute), but all in all, it's a great video, 59 seconds. Everyone gets to do a part of their own, and I think everyone is happy and excited. They all make my posters, we put on music and dance. Everyone is dancing and smiling and just all around having a great time. The most important thing is...I'M RUNNING FOR VICE PRESIDENT AND I COULD WIN! AHHHHHHHHHHHHHHHHHH!!!! (Now *that's* a happy scream.)

I think everyone of my friends will vote for me. I mean, these are my best friends. Why wouldn't they vote for me? I guess I am wrong. Maybe some of them aren't really my friends at all. Maybe one is just an imposter.

Chapter 2
Um...ok then

I notice something immediately the day the video is shown. I walk into the hallway feeling confident and happy, but everyone is looking at me differently than usual. I mean, I am not expecting people to applaud or anything, but this is just plain weird!

Makayla approaches me as I'm looking around the hallway. People are just staring at me. I've never been stared at like this. I don't like it.

"Hey Makayla, um, do you know why everyone is looking at me like this?" I look around yet again and gesture at the angry hallway with my hands. She doesn't seem to get my crazy gesture.

"Like what?" Makayla asks and walks away.

Suddenly, someone I don't even know approaches me. "Why didn't you listen to what she had to say in the video?" She looks generally sad. I want to shout, "I DON'T EVEN KNOW YOU!" But I don't shout. I can't, I'm in too much shock.

"What? What do you mean? I listened to everything. I mean, some things we had to cut out, but that was a time issue. Makayla had her own part." I answer. "You saw the video, didn't you..." I catch her name on the notebook, "Sammy."

"Oh." The girl walks away from me, but I am not entirely sure she is convinced. I mean, she ignored the entire last part of my speech. Well, actually, now that I think about it, the ignoring the last part of my speech is just rude.

The next class I have is history with both Ella and Crystal. I sit near Crystal and I ask her what is going on in the hallway. I'm still confused about it, and now I'm a little scared. Did Makayla say something bad about me? Crystal is not entirely sure, but she says it is something about Makayla. Oh, I knew it. It's Makayla. Oh, I am so angry with her right now. As I was about to answer back, class starts. I make a mental note to talk to her after class.

I don't actually get to talk to Crystal until lunch, in which I ask her what the heck did Makayla say? She answers that she isn't totally sure, but it can't be good. I feel scared and vulnerable suddenly, but I don't know why. I look over at Makayla, laughing and talking with Ella, my best friend. Is this something about her?

When I get home that day, I call my mom and take Peanut outside. I choose not to mention Makayla. It will probably all go away by tomorrow. Today was just overly confusing. I think everyone can agree with that.

It feels different the next morning when I get to school. I know everyone has stopped looking at me and has moved on to something else, but Makayla still shoots me evil grins. I don't know what is going on.

Is Makayla my friend? Or...isn't she?

I sit near Ella at lunch. She tells me about soccer practice, and I tell her about how excited I am to go to her house for halloween. I've been going there for Halloween since I was 7. I ask if anyone else is going and she shakes her head in reply. I smile for about a split second, but Makayla talks to Ella, and I eat my lunch in silence since Crystal is home sick.

When I get home, I realize I had a text from Crystal.

```
Hey Olivia
Hey Crystal r u ok
Yeah, just a cold i think
Thats good
My mom says I should b back in school 2morrow
Good. I was so bored in lunch
Didn't you have Ella
Yeah...but it's awkward sometimes
Oh. Sorry.
It's ok
When do they tell u if you 1 VP
Next Monday
Cool.
GTG
Bye
```

I feel great that Crystal will be back in school tomorrow. I don't even think twice about Makayla. Okay, I think twice. I think about it 50 times more than twice.

Chapter 3
Why People Didn't Vote for Me

I enter into math class the day after the commercials air. I've actually forgotten about yesterday in the hallway, though I'm not sure how. I sit at my assigned group with Eli Hansen (ran for president), Gracie Luck (not in student council), and Jared Meyers (not in student council) and Eli says something that surprises me. "I didn't vote for you, Olivia." I stare at him. I'm silent, because I really could care less about that. "Would you like to know why?" "No." I'm being honest. I, again, don't care. "I didn't like the ideas you mentioned. They seemed stupid." Really? I just told him I didn't care and...you know what, whatever. I'm not going to start a fight with Eli.

I stare at him again.

"Like the stupid one-"

"OK, Eli," I interrupt him. "I didn't ask if you voted for me. I didn't vote for you either, so I guess we are even." I try to be cool and confident, but inside, knowing that someone didn't vote for me because of my video hurts. I look around, questioning the trustworthiness of all my classmates.

Were they going to vote for me until they saw the video? Were they not going to vote for me in the first place? Were they someone like Eli who didn't like me and the video just made it worse? Needless to say, it is hard for me to concentrate in math class that day or any class, even lunch. How is it ever hard to concentrate in lunch? There is one goal: eat your food.

That's right, Eli isn't the only one who said that to me - so does Lela Meal, Brady Morris, Nadia Redmond, and Celia Banks. I don't tell my friends. They worked so hard on that video, so hard to make me happy, and I felt bad enough without saying anything. Why would somebody tell me why they didn't vote for me? Who the heck does that to somebody? I should tell them something

I don't like about them. Oh, there's plenty I can say. What to say, what to say...

That day, I take down all my posters in the hallway. They are only allowed to stay up until the afternoon after the election, which is today. When I walk out to the car, I think about what everyone said. Does this mean that I wouldn't win? How can you win when no one votes for you?

After my homework is finished, I text Ella. She doesn't answer me. I don't think twice about it. She is almost always busy at night, so I put my phone away and go to bed.

I am so glad it's Friday the minute I wake up. For one thing, it's officially almost Halloween. And another thing, Ella is sleeping over tonight. But I'm not as excited when I get to school and Makayla tells me about all the things her and Ella did the night before. So that's why Ella didn't answer!

"And then we played Wii."

'Yes, and then?' I'm getting extremely bored with this entire conversation. Like, seriously Makayla, is there a point to this or is it just to make me feel bad?

"And then we went up to her room."

"Oh, I am intrigued." I tune her out entirely until one comment. One that makes me specifically mad.

"I bet you never hang out with Ella and do the things we do together."

I was bored before, but now I am NOT!

"You know, since Ella likes me so much more."

I don't reply, but I don't bring it up at our sleepover. It doesn't exactly seem like the easiest topic, and besides, what happens if the truth actually hurts me? I mean, seriously, is what Makayla said about her and Ella true?

Chapter 4
Halloween Truths

So Halloween night finally comes, and I am so excited as I get in the car and go to Ella's house. George has to come with me, and he is hanging out with Ella's brother Mason, even though he is 11. Unfortunately, that means her sister, Hannah, is all alone and has to hang out with us. She is only 7. She can be kind of annoying, especially when Ella and I want some BFF time, like we do tonight.

After we get all our candy, we sort it out on Ella's rug. Then, all of a sudden, out of nowhere, Hannah goes, "Ella said Makayla didn't vote for you, Olivia. Is that true, because I thought you guys were friends. Is that true? Am I wrong about that? Is that true?" Hannah repeats herself most of the time, I'm used to that, but this time it feels different because of what she is saying. Makayla didn't vote for me? Why wouldn't Makayla vote for me? I thought we were friends. I am suddenly very, very confused.

Makayla was my campaign manager. She passed out cards that said "Vote for Olivia." At least, I think she did. Or did she lie about that too?

Ella looks very, very angry at her sister. Hannah gives a confused look, like "What did I say?" I look at Ella, who is very uncomfortable. "Is that true?" I ask. "Did Makayla not vote for me?" Suddenly, I feel like I'm being punched in the gut repeatedly. And then a dinosaur digs into my insides. And then I find out that my best friend hates me.

"Olivia. There is something I have to tell you. I don't think you are going to be happy about it." Ella still looks very uncomfortable, and looks like she wants to kill Hannah for even saying *anything*. Well, looks and talks like she wants to kill her. Ella has emphasized the "I" and is doing everything she can to show Hannah that that was not her secret to tell. I agree, except Hannah may have just done me a favor.

I glare at Ella. I guess I shouldn't be mad at her, but I kind of am. Why would she keep such a big secret from me? "Why wouldn't she vote for me?" I ask, using all my strength to stay in control. In reality, I want to punch something to get all my anger out before I explode into a million tiny pieces. I think I'm one step away from doing just that!

"I don't know. But you are going to win. We are going to show Makayla we don't need her vote!" Ella is trying to make me feel better, but inside, I just feel worse.

I know I'm not going to win. With so many people who know me not voting for me, there's no way people who don't know me will. I don't want to make Ella feel worse, so I just say, "Yeah, I'm going to win," as confidently as I can manage. Unfortunately, I'm not a very good liar, and Ella is very observant.

"I'm sorry. I shouldn't have said anything. Blame Hannah!" she looks at me. "Is something else bothering you?" she asks me. She's sincerely looking at me and I can tell she's concerned. But this isn't her life. It's mine with my problems and my things to deal with. It's my 7th grade nightmare, not hers.

"No," I lie, but fortunately, she doesn't catch this lie. I smile at her to seal the deal, when really I feel like crying or hitting something.

"OK. If you need to talk, you can always come talk to me Olivia." she smiles at me and right then I want to tell her everything so badly, everything about no one voting for me, but I keep my mouth shut. I just nod and smile. But it's fake; I can feel it and she can see it, but luckily she doesn't push anything.

I wave goodbye to Ella at about 10:00 pm. As soon as I get into the car, I tell my mom everything that Makayla did. She actually laughs at some of them.

"Oh, that is ridiculous," she says, "What kind of campaign manager doesn't vote for the person they are campaigning?" I glare at her. This is not funny. This is a serious matter, and I'm mad she doesn't think that.

"Obviously Makayla," I say. I don't feel like laughing. I'm really sad. I thought we were supposed to be friends. Friends don't do that to other friends. Does she hate me or something? What did I do? What did I ever do to deserve this. I feel like I've always been nothing but nice to her.

When I get home, I check my phone. Makayla texted me, but I ignore it. I don't feel like talking to her right now. I don't feel like it's worth it after what Ella brought to my attention. There goes my great Friday Halloween.

Chapter 5
Meanwhile in School

I still like all my classes. My teachers are all nice, and I still sit with my friends at lunch. Now that we've been in school for officially 2 months, my teachers all try to make us like it more because summer is officially over. Every Friday, they dance to a new song after school, and usually Crystal and I meet up at our lockers and laugh, although sometimes if we know the song, we sing along.

We get our progress reports and I'm getting all A's, which helps me toward my goal. I bring it home tell my parents to sign it, and bring it back. Other than that, some things aren't so great.

Makayla and I don't speak a lot anymore. I don't really know why, but it seemed to have started as soon as I knew about her not voting for me. It's really awkward at the lunch table sometimes. I want to stop this and get things back to the way they were before I knew her secret. Sometimes Ella doesn't even talk to me.

Now, I've gotten pretty close to Crystal. It feels different though. We have a line that separates our two tables. I used to sit next to Ella on one side of the line. Now, I sit across from Crystal on the other. I feel really bad sometimes. It's like I'm at a completely different table than my best friend.

November

Chapter 1
The Results are In!

I can't wait until the Monday that they tell us the winners for the positions in Student Council. Crystal is talking to me at our lockers, but I am barely listening. I'm too busy bouncing with fear and excitement to listen. I mean, who wouldn't be? I'm about to find out whether or not I won vice president. Probably didn't win. Why am I excited again?

"Olivia, what's going on with you? I mean, did you even hear a word I said?" Suddenly, she realizes what day it is. "Oh. Is this about the elections? Don't worry Olivia. Everyone at our lunch table voted for you, and you have Sierra and Natalie in younger grades." (Natalie is my friend in 6th grade).

I want to tell Crystal everything that Ella told me but I know I can't. I had promised her I would say nothing. I don't think I've ever regretted a promise more. If I could go back in time, I would tell past me to ignore what Ella says and just tell someone. But I can't. Now I'm paying the price for it. I sigh and nod as confidently as I can manage with my mouth sealed and the largest secret I've ever had to keep trapped inside of it. She gives me a hang in there smile and leaves for her advisory class. I sigh as I watch her go. She doesn't know what I'm going through and I'd like to keep it that way for as long as possible.

I walk into my class. I only have one friend in there. I thought I had another friend, but it turns out that I don't. It's Makayla. She doesn't sit with me today, so I end up sitting at a group of desks with Chloe, who luckily isn't mad at me. Now that I think about it, maybe I'm overreacting. Maybe everyone isn't mad at me. Maybe some people who aren't my friends still voted for me. You never know. Even if I don't win, it would still be nice to know that.

I can't wait for the announcements to come on! I want to know if I won so, so, so badly. No one else is as worried as I am. No one else is thinking, I want to win so badly! Let me win! PLEASE!!!!!!!!!!!!!! But maybe it's a good thing. Maybe the nerves are the universe's way of telling me that I am going to win. My stomach does a flip. Or maybe it's just an uncomfortable waiting position until I find out that I didn't win.

Finally, I hear the beeping signalizing the announcements are about to begin. "Good morning WRMS, please stand for the pledge of allegiance."

Everyone stands up, and I notice my knees are shaking big time. The pledge of allegiance continues and I mouth it absentmindedly. It's now or never. I know it is!

They go through a bunch of random, unimportant things like who won the softball game or that after school tutoring is that day. Why are the stupid announcements taking so long? I feel like when I'm not waiting for something they go by too quickly for me to get through even one chapter of whatever book I'm reading at the time. Then finally, they say the positions for student council. I immediately give the 8th graders that are speaking my FULL attention. This is it. I've been waiting since 5th grade for this one announcement. This could define my entire middle school experience. Well, up until the next thing happens.

"Please congratulate your new president, Eli Hanson, Vice President, Julie Roberts..." I don't even listen to the rest of what they say. Julie Roberts is in 5th grade! She may be nice, I saw her video, but you can't have a 7th grader as president, and a 5th grader as vice president. It doesn't make sense. I try not to sulk and mope around. I try to make sure I look happy, like "What? I wasn't running for vice president." I'm not sure how well that comes across.

The next class I have is history, which is the class that I have with Crystal. She gives me a sympathetic look. I nod back at her across the room, a silent sign that says, I'm okay. Even though, you know, I'm totally and absolutely not okay. I'm totally and absolutely depressed right now, but Crystal doesn't need to know that. She nods at me, her sign to say, Ok, good, then turns around. She believes the lying look.

I have student council that day. It takes all my concentration to not push Julie Roberts out of her chair. I just give her a smile, and sit with who I sat with last time. They all talk like they normally would. I just get out my phone and text my mom that I'm in student council, doing okay and that stuff. I don't feel like texting anyone, but I guess if I must, I'll text her.

I also tell her that I didn't win. She sends me a sympathy texts, if texts can include sympathy, and says my dad will be picking me up today. I text back all good.

After student council, my dad picks me up. "How was it?" He asks me. I shrug, not really in the mood to talk. He doesn't push it, and we ride home silently. I am so so so mad. I know this is all because of Makayla. So, needless to say, today has not been the best day for me so far...

Chapter 2
Group Work (Dun dun dun)

Mrs. Keller wants us to get better at "working with a group." Therefore, she starts us on group work. I really don't like group work. I think I can work all on my own, independently. I don't need a group behind me, because sometimes, they mess me up or make me get the wrong answer. Seriously guys, it's happened to me before. Trust me. Here, I'll prove it to all you non believers out there.

Here is a very accurate look into the world of Olivia and group work.

Me: Guys, I don't think that's the right answer. The right answer is everything happens for a reason. I am positive. Please just listen to me. Do you want to fail ELA for 7th grade? Because that's where we are headed right now.

Kaylee: It's definitely the right answer. *eye roll* Seriously.

Mayer: Stop worrying Olivia. It will all be fine. We've got the right answer. It's 3 against 1. Besides, we all read the same book. You've read a lot of books, so there is a chance that you're confusing the theme of this book with the theme of another one that you have read. (Tell me, please, does this make *any* sense to you?)

Me: Ok...I guess. But guys, are you sure? I mean, I seriously think that it's the wrong answer.

James: So, who wants to share out for the group? I'm definitely not doing it. I'm way too terrified of speaking in public. (James ignores me a lot)

Kaylee: Liv can! She likes sharing out! Don't you Liv? You know the answer that we came up with, right? Oooh! This is the best idea ever. (Sometimes Kaylee gives me a headache).

Me: Don't call me that. Guys, I seriously don't think that this is the right answer. I think the right answer is-

James: Olivia, please. Just do it. We're a group. Stop arguing. We're all going to get in trouble. Can you please just do it? I promise it's the right answer.

Me: (sighs) Fine, whatever. You guys win I guess.

Mrs. Keller tells the group speakers to stand up. I stand up confidently though I have no beliefs that what we are saying is anywhere close to the truth. DON'T PICK ME FIRST! DO NOT PICK ME FIRST! I AM WARNING YOU! IN MY HEAD I AM YELLING IN ALL CAPITALS TO NOT PICK ME FIRST! Look, over there, Sasha is standing up. She is really smart. Mrs. Keller smiles and picks me first. Great. Thank you so much Mrs. Keller. What would I do without you?

Ok, I'm about to make a bad impression, but maybe it won't be the worst thing in the world. Oh, who am I kidding? This is going to be absolutely awful. I know it is.

"I think..." Here, I swallow, knowing I am lying, "...the theme of the book is don't give up." Then I sit down, trying to block the traumatic experience out of my memory. It takes all my strength not to put my head in my hands and just cry right now. I want to sprint out of the school. I want to do anything I can to get out of this ELA class. I feel my face turn bright red, but I don't think people are looking at me enough to notice it. Or maybe they are. What if everyone is looking at me right now? That would be the absolute worst thing in the entire world.

My teacher looks almost shocked. "Actually, no Olivia. The theme of the book is everything happens for a reason." She looks around at the rest of the class. I swear I see Kelli whisper something to her best friend Julia, but I ignore it. Just like my groupmates ignored the fact that I was right and they were absolutely positively wrong about everything.

I want to look back at my groupmates and shout, "HA! I told you so!" but instead I sit down and simply say "OK." Mrs. Keller better not think that's what I thought the answer was. If she had been listening to any of the conversations that were previously had, she would know. I haven't even been in 7th grade 3 months and I was already making a bad impression.

OK Olivia, calm down, you're thinking WAAAAAAAY too much into this. She probably didn't even think twice about it. Unless, why did she look shocked? Why did she look at the rest of the class? Why did Kelli whisper to Julia? Well, I may have been hallucinating out of pure fear and embarrassment, but I don't think I was. Kelli whispered to Julia. Mrs. Keller looked shocked. I have just made a terrible impression, and there is nothing I'm going to be able to do about it except live out these two years until 9th grade, when things will hopefully things get better.

That's it. I am packing my bags. I am going to Africa. Wait, no, Africa's too far. Plus, there's ebola. Okay, what about...California. My cousins live in California. I never see them but I'm sure they'd love to see me everyday in school. Wait, um, no. They are all boys and I haven't seen them since I was, what, 6? That idea is out. How hard do you think it would be to convince my parents to let me switch schools? Yeah, that's what I thought.

After ELA, I speed walk, no, run out of the classroom. Yes, I break a rule, but in my defense, I want to get out of the environment of my wrong answer that wasn't even my fault as quickly as I can. To be honest, I never want to go back. I never want to come back to this school. I want to stay home. Maybe my parents can homeschool me. They're teachers. (Well, my dad is a guidance counselor, but he was a teacher for a while.)

You might think I am really overreacting. But, ask any of my friends and they will say that it is perfectly normal for me to be obsessing about something as stupid as me giving a wrong answer in class. I'm lucky I have lunch next. I grab my lunch box and glide into the lunch table next to Ella, who as usual, ignores me. I slide over to what seems to be my new normal spot across from Crystal. She raises her eyebrows at me. I roll my eyes in return. It's funny how well we can communicate just from looks. I don't think Ella and I have ever been able to do that. I mean sure, sometimes we think the same things at the same time, but never have I understood what she meant by a simple glance. It's weird that that's just with Crystal.

I tell Crystal all about my adventures in "group work". She smiles. "You're way too nice Olivia. Don't let them walk all over you. If you knew the answer, you should have made sure that if you were speaking you were giving YOUR answer, not theirs!" She actually pounds her fist on the table to make her point and I giggle and take a sip of my water bottle.

"I tried too. It's not exactly the easiest thing when it's 1 against 3. Plus, they think that I like speaking in public. I don't-not when I know that I'm actually saying the wrong answer. Unintentionally is one thing, but it's different when I know what the answer and I'm not allowed to say it. You don't know what that's like Crystal. I like it so much better when we can just work independently. It's very stressful during group work. You're so lucky to not be in that class," I say once I've put it down. Not one word of that whole rant was a lie. I mean all of it as much as it's possible to mean something.

Crystal smiles but doesn't really respond. I just shrug. I don't really care whether or not she answers. I've said what I feel I've needed to say. I've gotten it all out. As lunch ends, I walk to my next class, hoping there is absolutely no group work involved.

Chapter 3
The Boy in the Hallway

I walk into school thinking it's just going to be a normal, regular Friday. I am talking to Crystal at my locker and Ella's talking to Makayla, again. It's like she's obsessed with her or something. I roll my eyes. It's honestly a little creepy. No one's with a person that much unless they're in an unhealthy relationship or something. Which, if you ask me, is not the most unlikely thing.

Anyway, a boy walks into the yellow hallway. He's looking at his schedule with a panicked look on his face. I keep looking at him. He's kinda nice looking, I guess. Ok, why do my cheeks feel hot? I cannot get them back to normal temperature. I've never seen him before. Who is he?

Suddenly, he approaches me. I can feel myself turning bright red, but I don't know why. "Hey, do you know where I can find Mr. Lion's classroom? I have him for math."

I nod and point out the right place. I can't help but smile but I have no idea why. It's just a really weird morning I guess. He smiles, thanks me, and I turn back to Crystal, who has finished getting her books out of her locker. She looks at me like I have three heads. I think I'm still smiling, but I can't be too sure. I mean, I don't really know what's up with me. Maybe I'm sick or something. I definitely can't control what I'm doing right now.

"What is up with you?" she asks, looking me up and down. I guess I am still smiling and blushing. I shrug. Suddenly, Crystal gets a knowing look. "Oh. You have a crush, don't you?" She nods, smiling knowingly. I blush. Is this a crush? No. This isn't a crush. There's no way this is a crush, because I promised myself I would never like a boy. Liking a boy leads to a broken heart, and I don't want a broken heart.

I look at *her* like she has three heads now. "Why do you think I have a crush? I've never liked boys. Have you *ever* known me to like boys?" I ask her, raising one eyebrow. Well, I think I raise one eyebrow. I'm never entirely sure. I hope it comes across looking puzzled and a little bit like a detective. I am still blushing so I try to get my face back to it's normal color.

"Seriously Olivia, I know you have a crush. Hmm, who could it be?" she thinks for a second, looking up at the ceiling. "Is it that new guy, Jason? He's on my bus."

I shake my head, but inside, I'm really thinking about what she said. Is this what a crush feels like? My heart is racing, my cheeks are red, and I can't stop smiling. She tilts her head at me, as if trying to figure out if I'm lying.

"OK. See you in history," she says and waves goodbye. I wave goodbye too and walk to Mr. Lion's room while still smiling. It takes all my concentration to not start humming a random tune. I'm certainly happier than I was this morning. I want to ask Crystal a million more questions about this boy. I want to know everything about him!

Weird.

Wait.

Did that guy, Jason, say he was in Mr. Lion's class next? He's in my class? He's in my class. OK. Don't start panicking, Olivia. Everything will be FINE! Even though I know this, I check how I look in the bathroom mirror before I walk in. I look okay. Good. I mean, I never care how I look, but today is different. Today can't be different. I don't want to like a boy right now. Oh no. I'm getting myself way too deep into liking this boy, and I don't even really know who he is. He could be evil for all I know. I doubt that he's evil, but I don't know him. Anything is possible. Okay, I've officially lost it. The boy is not evil. I'm just trying to convince myself that I don't like him. Even though I think that may be the most impossible thing in the world. Why did my first crush have to occur right now? Today was going to be normal.

I walk in. Suddenly, I see him sitting in the seat that was empty next to me. Why oh why of all places did he have to sit there? I sit in my seat, smile in what I hope is not a creepy way, and put all my things into my desk. "Hey. I'm Olivia," I say, making sure I pay attention to every word I say. Don't want to accidentally blurt out that Crystal thinks I have a crush on him.

"I'm Jason. I just moved here from Connecticut. Not that far, but enough so that I don't know anybody here," he says. So Crystal was right, his name is Jason. Suddenly, I get the feeling that I got in the hallway. OK...I guess I do have a crush on him.

I can barely concentrate all math class with him sitting right next to me. Why does he have to be sitting right next to me? It's honestly like Mr. Lion wants me to make a fool of myself. I know he doesn't but it just really feels that way.

Anyway, I'm not going to tell Crystal about my crush. She would go all crazy! She'll try to talk to me about it, but I don't want to talk to her or anyone. I haven't even known this guy for an hour! But, that doesn't stop me from liking him, as much as I don't want to. I really don't want to like him.

As I walk out, he follows me to ELA. Then history. Then French. Then art. Is this guy in every class with me? It's as if the universe is just waiting for me to embarrass myself. Well, he's not in Chorus with me. He's in band. I wonder what instrument he plays.

Finally, it's the end of the day. Last block is gym. I have one more class to get through. "Hey Olivia," he says as he sits down next to me in our squads. I blush madly. Why am I blushing madly? I may as well have the words, "I like you Jason" tattooed across my forehead.

"Hey, um Jason. Hi. How were your other classes? Good? That's good. Yeah. So were mine." Smooth Olivia. Smooth. He wasn't even talking to me, and here I am, having a whole conversation with myself. Seriously Olivia? If you're going to talk to him, at least give him a chance to talk back to you. He probably thinks you're creepy considering you've have a full conversation with him this morning with no errors.

Suddenly, I realize that I'm staring. Noooooooooooooo. I force myself to look away. Before I get lost in thought, I should really look away from whoever I'm thinking about. Especially if it's Jason!

At the end of the day, my dad is at home. "How was school Olivia?" he asks me.

"Good," I say. "There was a new boy in class, Jason."

My dad smiles at me and I run up to my room to text Ella, who doesn't answer. I'm almost positive that she's spending the night at Makayla's house, just like she has been doing every Friday for the past month. Seriously, does she spend one Friday without her? I wonder who Jason used to spend his Friday nights with before he moved here.

Suddenly, I'm thinking about him again, (hopefully I can stop soon because it's starting to get really annoying) so I shake my head and turn on my favorite chanel to relax and stop thinking about him. Not that it works. I've gotta up my game with how I stop thinking about things.

When I've just accepted that TV is not working, I turn the TV off and just put on music. I've never done this before, but I'm interested to see if it works.

It does. It's like all my thoughts are being cleared from my head at one time, and I can think about one thing at a time. Suddenly, the whole Jason thing doesn't seem so bad. I just have to learn how to talk to him.

Chapter 4
6 A's and a B

The report cards are finally coming out last block today, the last day of November. First trimester is over. Done. I'm one third of the way done with 7th grade. Wow. It feels like just yesterday I started this and now here I am, three months in. Three of the longest, most confusing months of my life, but three months in still. I really think this should be considered a life accomplishment.

Anyway, the teachers have all updated our grades and I was rushing around so I forgot to check. I'm not worried. Right now, my lowest grade is a 90 in science class. All the others are high A's. (Except for one 91 in gym class, but that's not really my fault. I'm just not athletic whatsoever.) I did it! I actually achieved my goal! I thought it would be much harder than this.

I'm sitting in history, my first class of today, and the teacher hasn't come in. "I'm so so so excited to see my grades! I think I got straight A's!" I say to Crystal, who is sorting through her pencils. Don't ask me why. She looks up.

"Me too!" she squeals and we high-5. Suddenly, Jason comes up. Remember Jason? Well, it's been about a week, and I think I've gotten better at talking to him. He walks towards me, towards me, towards me...and right past me to sharpen his pencil. I try not to pout that he didn't come over especially to talk to me.

I look down at my mechanical pencil. Crystal's pencil is normal. I glance up at her. She's about to take out her pencil sharpener. What luck! "Crystal. Do you want me to go up and sharpen your pencil for you?" I ask her, smiling sweetly. I hope she says yes. This could be like the opportunity of the day.

"I can do it myself..." she starts. She looks down at her own pencil through her glasses. I shrug. She sighs. "OK. You can sharpen if you want." Crystal hands me the pencil. I leap out of my seat to see Jason sitting back in his own seat. I frown at the missed opportunity.

When I am done sharpening the pencil, I check on my unofficial countdown to last block. 6 hours, 53 minutes. I sigh as I hand Crystal her pencil. She thanks me and writes her name on the worksheet Mrs. Jack handed out. I write my own name.

The rest of the day goes by like the loser of a snail race runs a marathon. I don't know if that makes much sense, but it means slowly. Finally, I'm sitting in ELA, waiting to get my report card. I know what I got, but it will still be so so so awesome to see it on paper.

Jason gets his report card. "How'd you do?" I ask, making sure to concentrate on what I'm saying. Jason looks at me for a second before he starts talking to me. He's looking at me! He's actually looking at me and not looking the other way.

You know in the shows, books, and movies, people will try to find anything they can to show that the two characters like each other. That's how I am right now, except in this case, it's like I'm one of the two characters. I'm looking for any sign he likes me. Any sign!

"I've been here for a week. I don't even think they know who I am as a student yet Olivia. How do you think I'm doing?" he asks me. I try not to smile too big.

"You seem really smart," I say. Then, I blush. That sounded better in my head. Maybe I should stop talking to him entirely. You think that would work? I'm convinced. I'm never talking to him again. I've established a plan that won't work. I need to talk to him. How else is he ever going to like me back? Will he ever actually like me back?

He looks at me funny, mumbles a "thanks" and turns around to look at the board. I'm really mad at myself.

Finally, it's my turn. I think you should just see the report card I got for yourself. If I try to explain it to you...well, you'll see.

Hamilton, Olivia K

Math, Lion, Gordon-95-Olivia is a great student and a pleasure to have in class.

English, Keller, Jessica-97-Olivia is a great reader and writer who participates.

Language Arts, Keller, Jessica-98-Olivia is very good at vocabulary and words.

History, Jack, Emma-96-Olivia is showing good historical thinking skills recently.

Art, Mayer, Kara-100-Contact me at kmayer@kitkatmail.com to see my comment.

Chorus, Smith, Janey-100-Good job in class Olivia. Keep up the great work.

Science, Keddman, Hannah-89-See me about updating final exam Olivia. I need to talk to you about this. How about Wednesday after school?

Gym, Greyson, Jack-91-Olivia participates.

Chapter 5
And that's it for Trimester 1

My rating of 7th grade so far out of 10 is ... -2. It has been the weirdest, strangest, and the absolute most friendship testing year EVER! Are me and Ella still best friends? She hasn't exactly been talking to me the same. It's kinda been awkward. It should never be awkward with your best friend. Or maybe...I don't want to say it.

I'm starting to hang out with Crystal more though. She's much more awesome than I remember. In dance class when we were six, she almost never talked to me. I think it's because she was shy. Crystal's still sort of shy and doesn't like giving answers in class. But, she's definitely improved since we were first grade dancers. Plus, she's funny, nice, and smart.
Just like Ella.

She is almost exactly like Ella, whom I met when we were little preschoolers when she was the one who was always bouncing and talking to teachers. Little "Can't-sit-still" Ella with me in the background reading picture books. Or, rather, pretending to read, since I couldn't read until closer to my 5th birthday. Ella came up to me and said, "Do you wanna be my friend? I don't have any because people think I'm weird!" I just nodded and she grabbed my arm, and told me everything about her. "Now you tell me stuff about you!" I remember her demanding me. I just shrugged with my face heating up and thought, "This girl is going to be my best friend forever. Because she's too awesome to lose."

December

Chapter 1
Tara Jackson

It's early December. I'm waiting for the snow. Sledding, snowmen, snow angels...maybe for younger kids. For me, it's all about snow days. No school, even if I have to make it up later in the year, right now it's worth everything to me. Especially now in 7th grade, with all this drama. By drama I mean, the issue of why the heck isn't Makayla speaking to me. Anyway, I'm walking into school. I have to stay after today with Mrs. Keddman, my science teacher, to talk about my TCA (which means Trimester Common Assessment, it's like an exam that happens every trimester) that I felt so confident about. Needless to say, I'm not looking forward to that. I go to my locker. Suddenly, someone taps on my shoulder. "Excuse me?" I turn around, my hair whipping my face. I try not to wince. If it's never happened to you, take my word for it, it hurts. "Hi. I'm Tara Jackson. I'm new here. I couldn't help noticing your schedule. You have ELA next with Mrs. Keller? So do I. Is it okay if I walk with you?"

I nod, but inside I'm thinking, *Is this girl a spy?* She was looking at my schedule? Why is she looking at my schedule? I guess I can be nice to her. I mean, she is a new student and she probably doesn't have too many friends here yet. We walk down to Mrs. Keller's classroom. Turns out, she moved here from New Hampshire and with her old friends, she pretends to be a spy. Or, they think she pretends. I doubt she's actually a spy, because I don't think spies can reveal that, especially not to people they just met.

"You're on my street right?" she asks. "I saw you walking down to the bus stop today. Asher Rd? I live two houses down from you. You should come over after school." She smiles at me, revealing her no braces teeth. I run my tongue over my own braces. She has the ability to be super popular, considering he golden brown hair and perfectly straight white teeth. Maybe she is a spy.

I nod. Then I remember my previous after-school plans. "I have to stay after with Mrs. Keddman today. Maybe after." I've already filled her in on all the teachers. She nods excitedly and we walk into ELA.

School goes by quickly, and before I know it, I'm sitting in Mrs. Keddman's classroom. "So, Olivia, I would like to talk to you about your final exam." She shows me my grade and it's like a punch in the gut. In red pen, a big 67. The TCA I studied so hard for, a 67? I just shake my head. "Olivia, I know you know the material. Did you forget to study?"

I shake my head no. "I studied. The test was just much harder than I expected. I'm sorry. Can I retake it?

"Sorry. All grades are final. Remember, you're in 7th grade. But, I can give you some extra work. Not for a grade, but for an extra practice. Just believe in yourself Olivia."

I nod and she dismisses me. I walk out to the car with tears stinging my eyes. I don't talk to my dad on the way home. I just stare out the window. I can't wait to see Tara.

When I get out of the car, I look for the house that has been empty for as long as I can remember, and I see two cars parked in the driveway. I walk up to the door and ring the doorbell and Tara answers it as if she had been waiting next to it since school ended. "Hey Liv," she says, and I'm too annoyed with Mrs. Keddman to correct her right now. I don't know if I've said this yet, but I hate being called Liv.

"Hey Tara," I answer. She leads me into her house. It's pretty huge, and there are boxes everywhere, yet not enough to distract me from the size of the house.

This is honestly like a mansion! How does she not appreciate this?

"I'm not unpacked yet, but this is the kitchen, this is the living room, this is the bathroom, and this is my brother's bedroom," she says, leading me around quickly. I nod. "But this, Liv, is the main thing I wanna show you. Come on!" I follow her down a narrow hallway.

"This is my bedroom. The Tara Zone! It's the only room in the house that is completely finished since we moved in this weekend. Isn't it cool?" I nod again. It is pretty amazing.

The walls are a lavenderish color but they seem to have a tint of blue in it too. Her bed is white and black and full sized with a gray comforter with light blue and lavender stripes on it. Then, in another corner, there is a window seat, complete with a dark purple cushion. Then, all around her room, there are canvases covered in hearts, stars, and sayings. That's all she has besides the normal dresser and nightstand, but it's still pretty amazing for, what, three days? I am honestly in awe. She blushes as she catches me looking around. "So, wanna go play spies now?"

"Sure," I say, and we rush outside. The grass is extremely green. Seriously, how much did they pay for this house? Because I'm willing to offer the Jackson family double what they paid. This place is seriously amazing. She doesn't have anything in her backyard yet, but it's still pretty big. We start playing as soon as she explains the rules to me. It's simple really. All you have to do is hide somewhere, and the other person has to avoid obstacles. It's like a tweenage version of the game hide and seek.

Before I know it, it's almost 7 and my parents are calling me inside for dinner. Tara and I are practically on the floor laughing about stuff that no one else would understand. I wave goodbye and walk back to my own house.

Maybe this whole Ella thing was fate. Tara seems pretty cool, nice, and funny. She seems like a loyal person. Isn't that what a best friend is supposed to be?

Chapter 2
What I get for thinking life is good...

It's George's 10th birthday. It is otherwise known to me as: Today is a normal Monday in which I will have to go to school and see Ella, Makayla, Crystal, Jason and all the other people. Then we will go out for dinner. That is, if George doesn't complain about where we have to go on his birthday.

Don't get me wrong. I love that my little brother is getting older. I mean, next year he goes to middle school and I honestly couldn't be more excited. It's just sometimes I don't want him to grow up. I'm only 12. I mean, Lexi's brother is only 3 and he is so adorable. He can barely talk. And George, well, George is 10. George can talk. George is not 3.

I'm talking to Crystal and Tara at lunch today. Tara is a really a fun person to sit with and talk to, and we have gotten a lot closer since her first day. They both already know about George. (Crystal's known me since we were 6; Tara's already been at my house twice) I'm telling them how he's 10 today. Crystal's sister, Alexa, is 9 and in George's class. She says that her sister likes George. I think that's weird. I've only had a crush for not even a month, and Alexa already has one? Besides, why of all people does she have to have one on George? My brother? Why do people have crushes on my brother? That's uncalled for.

Anyway, they mostly tell me stories about their siblings. Alexa and her friend Beth slept over at Crystal's house and Crystal couldn't sleep the whole night. They were up laughing and talking and watching movies, leaving Crystal sleepless. Evan, Tara's 16 year old brother, had his friends Steven and Logan from their old school over to watch a baseball game, and Tara wasn't even allowed to have her old friend, Erica, over. She says she just sat in her room and listened to music, texting Erica the entire time. Even though I can't relate, I just roll my eyes and groan with them. It seems like the right thing to do in this situation.

Lunch, however, seems longer than normal. It drags on. Usually I'm wishing it was never over and I had more time to talk with my friends, but today's different. I guess it tends to drag lately since everyone from one side of the table doesn't really include the other side anymore. Sometimes I just watch them. Other times, I read. Some other times, I just try to get involved in the conversation. The last option almost never works, but that doesn't stop me from doing it. I'll try anything.

Today has been a slow watching day. I am relieved when I see Chloe come over to our table. She sits down across from me. When she says hello, I can hear the sadness in her voice.

"What's wrong?" I feel obligated to ask. Worst mistake ever. Couldn't I have just found out when she wasn't in advisory next Thursday?

"I'm moving," she answers. "Next Wednesday."

My heart pounds. The one advisory friend I have, gone. And Makayla's not going to talk to me, and it's just going to be awful. But this is for Chloe. I have to at least try to help my friend feel better, no matter how upset I am right now. I am really, really, really upset. Why does she have to move? Doesn't she know what will happen in advisory if she does? But I have to stay strong for my friend. I can't imagine she's super happy about it either. "That's terrible Chloe! Why are you moving? Why is it so sudden?"

She just shrugs and I feel like an awful friend for not doing anything. I just sit there and watch. You may be thinking, Olivia, stop being a jerk and hug her or something. But no, I just sit there. Some friend I'm turning out to be. After two minutes of me just sitting there doing nothing, Chloe gets up and leaves. Crystal and I look equally shocked. "I can't believe she's moving," I finally say, looking at my friend. I think we are both in a sort of shocked daze right now. At least I'm not the only one.

Crystal just nods. I get up silently, throw my garbage away, and ask for a pass to the bathroom. The teacher gives it to me and I go inside one of the stalls. It's quiet in here and actually sort of peaceful. People don't want to waste their precious lunch time pretending to use the bathroom when they're really just fixing their makeup or whatever it is they do in here. They don't go to the bathroom is all I know.

I don't know why I came in here exactly. I think it was mostly to get away from all the noise so I can think. OK. OK. Chloe's moving. I have one last advisory class until it officially becomes my worst class ever. Well, besides gym. Nothing is worse than gym. Yay.

I thought life was actually going okay. I don't have to deal with Makayla as much anymore now that she completely ignores me for Ella. Ella has not been ignoring me quite as much, but still enough, but I don't really care. Then this has to go and happen.

I didn't hate advisory. Besides history, it was the one class I could actually stand. I get to talk to Chloe, who was so busy after school and in her other classes that I barely get to talk to her. Besides, today is going okay. Or I guess was going okay until I found out the horrible news.

As usual, I am the first one home after school. I call my mom and she says she'll be home in about 30 minutes, so I call my dad. He says he had to stay after school for a meeting and he'll be home in about an hour. I don't know how this day took such a turn for the worst. I groan and flop on the couch. I don't want to go back to school tomorrow, not when I know what my school day is going to be like. Not when I know I only have a little while before I officially hate advisory forever.

I hope George had a great 10th birthday, because my day was absolutely, without a doubt, terrible!

Chapter 3

Sitting Alone...with April

You should probably get comfortable, because today is the absolute most confusing day. It was weird, crazy, and I wouldn't be surprised if it were National Let's-Make-Olivia-Feel-Like-An-Advisory-Loser day. Yep. It's that day. Chloe moved away.

Wednesday is not terrible. It could have been better, but Chloe isn't in school, and we all miss her, but it's like, hey, at least Christmas Break is coming up soon! I think today is probably the day when my world came crashing down. Today I felt like a bigger middle school outcast than normal.

I walk into advisory today. Where do I sit? Where do I sit? Please, somebody help me out here! I know it's not the best situation, sitting with me, even though I don't know why. But the only friend I had in advisory moved away and now I have no one. I finally find a seat next to Mimi. Hey, Mimi, we're not the closest friends but...

She gets up and she walks away. Seriously? Who does that? I slump my shoulders in defeat and look for somewhere else to sit. Everywhere is taken. Come on, somebody, make a spot for me. There is absolutely nowhere. OH NO! I am *not* going to be Olivia "Sits by Herself in Advisory" Hamilton. I desperately look around. There is nowhere else I could possibly sit. THIS CANNOT BE HAPPENING! I'm desperate. Okay. Don't freak out. No one is even looking at you. You'll be fine.

I WILL NOT BE FINE! I try to shrink myself into the desk as far down as I possibly can. This cannot be every advisory class can it? I quickly scan the room one more time before I just take out a book, hoping no one is looking at me and thinking I am the crazy weird girl with no friends. Or, the girl who cannot make any more friends. Or, the girl who thinks she's too cool for everyone else in advisory. If they think that, they obviously don't know me, because I'm not what you would call one of the cool girls. I don't think I'm even in the top 100.

Maybe I could get switched into Crystal's advisory class. I believe she's with Tara. I hear chatters behind me but I don't look up from my book. I don't even listen to what they're saying, I mostly just try to tune them out. I feel my face turn bright red but I think I may possibly be overreacting. This isn't that bad is it? No, no it is not that bad. However after reading over the sentence I'm on about 50 times, I still can't figure out exactly what it says. I roll my eyes and shut my book. I am going to need some serious help if the first bell hasn't rung yet and already I feel friendless.

I take out my agenda book and scan through it. There's a lot of interesting stuff here that I never bothered to read. I read it a little bit, realizing it's actually more interesting than my choice silent reading book. It doesn't even hit me that I've reached such rock bottom that I am reading the *agenda book.* Someone taps me on the shoulder and I look up innocently. Please don't be here to make fun of me. Please. That's not what I need right now. What I need is a friend, so if you're here to make fun of me, just remember that. Now, speak.

"You're reading the agenda book? Cool!" she says. I can't say I've ever met her, but she sits next to me so I smile. "I'm April." She hold out her hand. I shake it weakly. "This is my last day in this advisory class. I'm getting switched to the other team after Christmas break."

"Cool," I say. She seems nice enough, almost potential friend material, but she's getting switched to the other team. I wanna talk to her, but it's an awkward silence. Maybe this is why I have trouble making new friends. I don't know what to talk about. Luckily, she does.

"So, I have this dog, his name is Freddy and he is so adorable. Do you have a dog?" I open my mouth to answer but she's already on a completely different topic. "I need glasses to see distances. Do you need glasses?" I try to answer again, but she's talking again. I need to learn not to answer. "My highest grade right now is an 81. That's why I'm going to switch, because the teachers aren't able to teach me what I need to know. What's your highest grade?" I don't even open my mouth this time. I know she's not done. "I love reading but I'm terrible at it. It's hard for me to comprehend the words sometimes. I think I have some sort of reading disorder. Do you?" I shake my head, but I'm not sure she even notices. Does this girl ever stop talking? "Yeah, well, you should come over my house sometime. I see you all the time in class, but I'm usually too shy to talk to you. But since today's my last day...." she keeps talking. Her? Too shy to talk to me? Somehow, I doubt that. She's pretty talkative and I'm not cool. At all. Not even a little bit. I think we've been over this before actually. "Anyway, do you wanna come over my house sometime?" I shrug. This is like a one sided conversation. Suddenly the phone rings.

"April, you're needed at the office," the teacher says. Saved by the phone. She gets up.

"I'll be back as quickly as I can. I can't wait to get back to talking to you," she squeals and walks out. I want to move seats but I feel like that'll be rude. I mean, she seems nice, but one conversation and already I'm exhausted. I have no choice but to sit there and wait for her. I start drawing in my agenda book.

She comes back quicker than I expected. "Hey Liv!!!"

That's a little personal, I want to say. Not even my friends call me Liv because I don't let them. "Hey April."

We keep talking. Well, she keeps talking. I sit there, listening, wishing I was absolutely anywhere else, even sitting by myself. She seems nice just very talkative. Maybe the teacher will start talking. Maybe a fire alarm will blare. Maybe an asteroid will hit earth. Maybe aliens will attack. Maybe...

I just realized how crazy my ideas are.

I look at the clock. This block ends at 8:25 am and right now, it's 8:01 am. Twenty-four more minutes of April. How does anyone deal with this 24/7? From her talking, I learned she used to be homeschooled. I wonder why they sent her to school.

OK, I'm not usually that mean to people, but I have just been having a bad day. You would understand if you ever had a friend move away and left you with a person who wouldn't stop talking. Or couldn't stop talking, as in was physically unable to stop talking.

Finally, finally, finally, the clock turns to 8:25 am. I jump out of my seat when the teacher dismisses us. I am seriously considering getting switched into another advisory class. How hard do you think that would be to do? Because I am not dealing with April and no Chloe. Plus, I'll be pretty much sitting by myself when April leaves. I love to read, but it's not something I want to be doing while everyone else is with their friends.

I wish more than ever that I was even just a little bit popular, which is probably the wish of every single middle school girl, even though almost none of them have their dreams come true. Don't deny it. But unlike every middle schooler, I know I probably have no chance of becoming popular, unless I want to change everything about myself, which I don't want to do. Because most of the time, I'm happy being me.

My next class is history. Realizing I have it in the same classroom, I sigh and turn myself back around. Chloe is usually there to remind me that we have history in the same room after advisory when I jump out of my seat.

Crystal and Ella smile and wave as they sit down near me. Jason walks in the room, making my heart beat at the speed of light. How is it that one boy can do this to me? How is it that Chloe moving away can make me a friendless weirdo? How is it that people survive middle school?

Finally, after the longest, weirdest day ever, I get on the bus to go home. Sierra must see my face because she just says, "Bad day?"

I nod. "The weirdest day ever." Then, I start telling her all about how Chloe moved away. I leave out the part about me trying to talk to Jason during lunch but no words would come out. That was embarrassing.

"That stinks," she says, and she tells me something funny. We both laugh and for the first time all year, I feel like I have someone who understands. Crystal doesn't understand my life and neither does Tara. Ella definitely doesn't understand. She seems to have a perfect life where people don't disappoint her. It's about time something goes MY way.

Chapter 4
Two Friends and a Lie

I walk into Crystal's house for my first sleepover there. We squeal excitedly. Christmas was two days ago and there are ten days left of vacation. This is going to be a great sleepover. I can tell. I leave my duffel bag on her kitchen floor right next to my shoes, and say goodbye to my mom and brother.

We rush up to her bedroom. I sit on the mattress she pulled out for me while she sits down on her bed. "So, what's going on with you and Ella?" she starts. I knew she was going to ask me. But I can't answer because I don't even know.

"I don't want to gossip. I mean, me and Ella are still best friends so what's there to talk about?" I ask. Please don't go any further into this conversation. I'm not sure I can answer her. How am I supposed to talk about it when even I'm not entirely sure what's going on?

She shrugs. "Well, all she ever does is hang out with Makayla. It's like she never has time for you anymore. You guys have been almost inseparable since you were 4, right?"

"I guess," I say. I can't help but think about when we were 5 and made up our own secret language that no one else could understand. Or when we were 7 and stayed up almost all night, laughing and talking over a TV show even though we were exhausted and had waaaay too much candy. We had a sleepover almost every Friday night for a year when we were 10, meaning that we didn't get a whole lot of sleep in 5th grade. How were we supposed to? It's called a sleepover, but everyone knows you don't actually sleep. We were inseparable! "But we're still best friends. We just aren't little kids anymore. We're 12 now. Well, she's one month away from 13. But still." That was just about the most confusing thing I've ever said, but Crystal either understands or has something to say to add onto the confusion and gossip.

"She said you two aren't friends anymore."

"What?" I ask, feeling the tears form in my eyes. I didn't want to gossip. Someone always gets hurt and that someone is usually me. I can't help it though. Now I need to know what happened. I wish I didn't. I don't want to. But I have to. Why doesn't my best friend want to be my friend anymore? Was it something I did? I try so hard never to hurt her, but I must have, someway, somehow. I just don't know. "Why?"

Crystal just shrugs her shoulders which for some reason really annoys me. "She just said, 'Me and Olivia used to be best friends, but I guess middle school changed us. We aren't really friends anymore.' I don't know. I overheard her talking to Makayla about it. You can ask Makayla."

I don't need to ask Makayla. I trust Crystal, the only person I know who never lies. Well, other than Ella, I guess, but Ella lied. How am I supposed to trust what she says? I mean, Ella has her tell, but if she does her tell, doesn't that mean that she is lying? It does, I guess. I'm not sure I want to know. Besides, I guess it makes sense. I almost never have the same fun time with Ella that I always have. I text her.

`Els, are we still best friends?`

She texts me back immediately. My phone beeps, but I'm not sure I want to read it. It beeps again. I sigh and turn it on, wincing as I slide open my phone and type in my passcode.

`Of course Liv!`

No. No. NO! She's lying. She only calls me Liv when she's lying about something. That's her tell. I shake my head. It can't be. I don't know why I didn't believe Crystal. I don't know why I had to see for myself. Now, I have tears in my eyes and Crystal is looking at me with a sympathetic look on her face. She kneels down and hugs me. Crystal is saying, "You still have me and Tara. Two amazingly great friends. Who needs Ella? She's a jerk if she doesn't want to be your friend anymore. Besides, aren't I your best friend too?"

"Yeah, but...I don't know. I thought me and Ella were so strong that nothing could tear us apart."

"Almost no friendship could survive forever. Me and Lizzy didn't make it past 5th grade. I got through it. And you will get through this. Is Ella really worth it Olivia? How great of a friend is she? Is she really worth all the stress that she's caused you this year?"

I shrug, but inside, I'm thinking, Ella is a great friend. She's totally worth it. I would do anything for Ella. And maybe, just maybe, she'd do anything for me.

Yep. What a great sleepover.

Chapter 5
So, jealous yet?

So, it's almost the end of the year. In fact, today is December 31st. I haven't exactly gotten over the whole "Ella" thing. Usually, I ask my mom if I can invite her over on new year's eve, but today, I asked my mom about Tara and Crystal. Tara's coming over at about 9 and leaving at midnight. Crystal is leaving a little bit later. Ella would usually sleepover, but with Tara and Crystal, I think I should take it one step at a time.

Anyway, overall, this month has been a crazy success. My teachers like me, I think. Makayla hasn't been speaking to me. Ella has still been speaking to me. Sometimes though, I wish she wasn't. I'm still really angry at her. I don't ignore her, that would be rude, but it feels more awkward now. Crystal feels really bad and is trying to make me feel better about Ella. It's not working. I haven't told anyone that Ella doesn't want to be my friend anymore. It's not really something you talk about.

I bet you really want this to be your 7th grade year. I know I'm really enjoying it!

January

Chapter 1
A Tale of Two Lunch Tables

The first day back at school after Christmas break is also a first for two other things. First for new friends and first for crazy ridiculous things that make absolutely no sense at lunch time. Right now, I'm going to talk about the crazy ridiculous things that make absolutely no sense at lunch time. Because now, we have two lunch tables. The responsible and irresponsible side. And guess which one I'm on. The irresponsible side. Ding ding ding, we have a winner, and one loser. Olivia Kiara Hamilton.

I don't understand it really. I come back from a sick day and decide to sit next to Ella. "Hey Els," I say. I'm still mad at her for saying that we aren't best friends anymore, but maybe being nice can help bring our status back up to friends. Suddenly, she's giggling and I'm sitting there, feeling like an idiot for not knowing what is going on.

"Move irresponsible!" Jenny yells. I give her a strange look, like what the heck is an irresponsible, but everyone is looking at me and Ava is even pointing to my "assigned side". I didn't know I have an assigned side! Why am I irresponsible? Why do we have to make this crazy? If I could tell them that Ella convinced me to scream all the way down the street once when we were 9 and we both got in trouble, I guarantee she would be right there, sitting next to me on the irresponsible side.

I look at Ella, my questionable best friend, for support but she's laughing her little heart out with Makayla. Makayla is laughing and pointing, I hate Makayla. It's mean, I know, but it's true! It's how I feel! Tears of sadness, fear, and anger sting my eyes as I move to my own side. "You okay?" Crystal asks.

I shake my head. I'm afraid if I talk I'll start crying and I am not cry-baby Olivia. I just start eating my lunch. I see Crystal staring at me but she doesn't say anything. I glance over at my former BFF. What happened Ella? What happened to you? Why does it seem like you've changed? You used to be amazing, but now, I'm not so sure. We used to be inseparable, and you even said you didn't want to deal with Makayla. Remember how mean she was to you in 3rd grade? Remember how you came to me crying because Makayla got you in trouble? Did she brainwash you or something? But Ella's not a mind-reader, so of course she doesn't answer the questions I asked her in my head.

Ella used to be the one to stand up for what she believed in, even if sometimes no one agreed with her. Ella used to be the nicest girl in school, the girl everyone wanted to be friends with. Ella was the girl with a smile that could light up an entire gym if she tried hard enough. Every smile was trying hard, and every smile was the same happiness. Ella used to be my best friend even though she was definitely able to find a prettier, and smarter friend than me. Ella had the potential to be popular and leave me. She still does. Now, she's using it for some reason. Is something going on with her?

And that's when it hit me. Makayla was prettier. Well, that could potentially be because she was always waking up 20 minutes earlier on weekdays to brush her hair and style it and she has to put a product on her face or something because it's always clear. And she was smarter, always coming into lunch saying she got a 100 on her latest test. But I never thought Ella cared about any of that. I thought she was happy with me. I thought we were going to be best friends forever and ever because nothing could ever break us up. I guess I was wrong.

I realize I've been staring at my sandwich instead of eating it so I take a bite. At the end of lunch, Crystal fills it all into me. I think she's trying to be gentle. Maybe she thinks I'm fragile or something right now. I mean, I guess I am, but who wouldn't be fragile when your friends say you can't sit next to them at lunch? They are joking around, saying they are responsible because they don't leave their friends. She says they think they are funny, but to me, they just sound like mean girls in a TV show.

When did this whole eating lunch thing become so complicated? Why can't I just sit down and enjoy my lunch? You know what? I know exactly why. It's because of Makayla. I'm positive she's behind everything. Because what isn't she behind. When's the last time something bad happened and it was Ella's fault? Nothing. Ella's never gotten in trouble in her life, except for that one time in 3rd grade, but that was Makayla's fault. Because Ella is the sweetest, nicest, most awesome person in the world, even though right now I'm not so sure.

The lunch bell finally rings and I race out to my locker. Ella taps me but I don't turn around. I'm not talking to her. I'm angry. I just head off to Chorus to see Brianna and forget about the whole lunch table thing for a little while. I'm not sure how much longer I can handle this madness. I leave Ella at my locker, but I don't even bother looking back at her. But a feel a pang of guilt knowing that I've made her feel bad, but only a pang. She made me feel so much worse today at lunch and this isn't even close.

It's nice, as always, talking to Brianna, but soon Chorus is over and I have to head to history, which stinks. Usually, it's my favorite class, but the thought of seeing Ella right now just makes me want to be sick. I sit at my assigned seat right near her and face the front. She comes in quickly after me. I know she's rushing to my seat, but I face front and cross my hands on my desk. She doesn't need me right now. I know she'd rather be laughing with her new best friend, Makayla. Ella's independent, confident, and, according to Makayla, responsible. I'm unconfident, immature, and irresponsible.

I've been holding her back. I've been holding everybody back with my immaturity and awkwardness. I just need to stop talking to everyone, keep my feelings inside. No one will even know. Whenever I'm mad, I can't show it. People will think I'm a crybaby. If I tell them what I watch and listen to, they'll judge me. I'm not making any more mistakes. This is middle school. I need to keep to myself. I don't even realize when Jason sits down right near me, that's how angry I am.

"Come on Olivia! Just say one word. Please," Ella begs. I look over at her. I don't feel like talking, but I know I have to talk. Otherwise, Ella will start telling people I'm giving her the silent treatment. And they don't need to think I'm a terrible best friend that gives people the silent treatment. I'm supposed to be gaining popularity. Not losing it. But maybe now isn't the best time to talk.

She's standing here, and I guess I feel like I should talk to her.

"Look Ella. I'm sorry about this, but you hurt my feelings. We're supposed to be best friends, but you won't even let me sit near you. You laughed at me! And to be honest, you haven't been yourself since you started hanging out with Makayla. But, maybe this is the real you you didn't want me to see. Maybe it's best if we just talk outside of school," I hear myself saying. I regret it the second it leaves my mouth. That's the meanest thing I've ever said to her. I feel awful, but I think it's too late. The poison has hit her. That regret turns into relief soon though.

I catch Ella's hurt face but I don't care. I feel victorious. Like nothing can ever stop me. But at that moment, the truth hits and I miss my best friend. My best friend who is walking back to her seat, about to cry, because of something that I said. I've never made my best friend cry before. Am I that horrible of a person?

OK, I'm back to feeling awful.

Chapter 2
All it Takes is Sorry...Unless it's Ella

The next day, the first thing I do when I walk into school is apologize to Ella. I never should have said any of that stuff yesterday, and she needs to know that. She needs to know I want things to go back to the way they used to be.

The funny thing is, the second I do it, I feel better. And she does too. She gives me a hug and says, "It's okay Olivia." I hug her back, and she says that she never really liked Makayla, and she was only doing it because she felt bad that Makayla has no other friends. I, of course, believe her, because she's nice like that, and I know what it's like to feel like you have no other friends. She invites me over for a sleepover that night, and I of course, accept. Things go back to normal and we live next door to each other for the rest of our lives, and our kids are best friends too. Everything is back to perfect, and it's like 7th grade never even happened.

Yeah, did you believe any of that? I wouldn't either.

Want to know what really happened? I have to warn you though, it's not all lollipops and rainbows. It's the cold, hard truth, that actually hurt me a little bit.

She just ignores me. She's trying to hide her anger, but that's bothering me. Ella knows all my weak spots. And this, her trying to hide how she is feeling is one of them. That's one of the many, many, many, *many,* problems with fighting with someone you've known since you were four years old. Some others include the silent treatment, and the fact that this is your best friend and now she absolutely, without a doubt, *hates* you.

"Ella, how can I fix this?" I ask. After thinking about it some more last night, I realized that I was partially in the wrong. She doesn't try to hide how angry she is anymore. She has a mean face. Oh no. I think that there's a chance that I might have possibly said the wrong thing here. And by chance, I mean, that is exactly what happened. Do I need to point out that I'm in trouble now?

"Olivia, I think the saddest thing here is that you don't even care about my feelings until I'm mad at you. I have been mad at you all night, not just when I knew you were mad at me. You can't make it better. At least not right now. I just need sometime." Ella turns into her locker and does her combination. I sigh, shoulders slumping in defeat and walk to my own locker. Tara is waiting there. I don't feel like talking to anyone right now, and I'm way too upset for peppiness. But, Tara's my friend, so I'm quiet and plaster on a fake smile, that I know looks way less cheery than my normal smile, but I don't really care about that right now. All that's running through my head is, *I need to fix things with Ella. Because if I don't have a best friend, what do I have? I have nothing. Without a best friend, I have the equivalent of nothing.*

"Hey Liv!" she squeals, waving. I wave back. I realize I still haven't corrected her on my nickname. Oh well. I'm too sad to correct her today. "Is it okay if my new friend, Mimi, sits with us at lunch today?" She's still bouncing. I'm usually that peppy. I could fake it, but I really don't want to. But, I feel like I have to fake it. I start bouncing a little bit too.

No, I think. *After everything that has happened with Ella today, no, it's not okay if she sits with us.*

Besides, Mimi hates me. Out loud, I say, "Yeah, sure, that's cool with me." I nod to top it off. In fact, I smile, keep bouncing, and giggle. I really don't want to make it seem like I'm upset right now.

"Awesome!" Tara squeals. Wow, this girl squeals a lot. She leaves for her next class and I leave for science. As I enter, I see Jason sit down at his assigned seat next to me. My cheeks heat up and I know that a blush is rising up my face. My whole head is screaming, "JASON ALERT! JASON ALERT!"

"Hey Olivia, what's up?" he asks. He's totally cool.

"Hi...um...stuff. Yeah. That sounds like a real answer. Cool." Smooth Olivia. Smooth. He's going to think you're a total idiot if you keep talking to him like that. I'm already blushing. He's going to know that you like him if you talk stupidly too. Well, he's going to know more so than usual. I hope I didn't sound ridiculous. Jason nods with a confused look as his face and I slouch down in my seat and look ahead.

I'm totally not cool. Maybe I can practice with George or something tonight. Wait, no, I can't tell him that I like Jason. I can't tell anyone that I like Jason.

After math class, I hear some bits and pieces of girls as they talk while I walk to my locker. "Yeah.....hideous.....did you see.........wearing? So.......I want..............yeah! Totes........ha, you're................" I roll my eyes. Nothing worth listening to. It's all about outfits, I think, plus it's all in whispers. I'm not going to start straining my ears to hear other people being talked about. I wonder if they know that it's them. I sigh slightly. It's crazy what 12 (and 13) year old girls will talk about. Seriously, other people's outfits?

Wait. I'm other people.

I slowly look down at my outfit and wish I hadn't. I'm wearing a purple t-shirt that includes a black sparkly peace sign with black yoga pants. It's my favorite outfit but it doesn't seem right for a 7th grader. What if I'm the girl they're talking about? While I grab my books, I grab my sweatshirt too. Just red, so there's no sequins or anything. This sweatshirt is safe. I'm lucky I caught that when I did.

Now I look acceptable. I zip up the sweatshirt and walk into my science class, hands in my pockets. I see another girl as she walks by talking to her best friend. I can't help hearing the conversation that they have. I don't know how with all the noise in the hallway. Maybe it's just something the universe wants me to hear.

"So, did you hear? Kim likes Jason! I was like, 'Kim, you should go ask him out' and she did and he said yes!" I hear Girl 1 say. I think there's also a squeal in there, but I ignore it. Why I keep listening, I don't know.

"OMG! They make a totes cute couple!" Girl 2 says. She squeals too, this time I hear it. "Where are they going on their first date?"

"I don't know. They might not even be going on a date, but since Jason is dating Kim, it's like the entire school will be talking about it sooner or later. I mean, how could they not?" It's back to Girl 1. She's the quieter one of the two.

"That's soooo romantic!" Girl 2 gushes. I want to shout, "No it isn't!" but I keep my mouth shut. An important part of eavesdropping is not letting people hear you there.

Kim? Suddenly, I know the name. Kim Brenton. She's the most popular girl in 7th grade. I don't stand a chance, especially if they're already dating. I want to talk to Ella, but then I remember that she's not speaking to me. She also doesn't know about Jason. How did this happen?

Chapter 3

Happy Birthday Crystal!

It's one day away from Crystal's birthday. I've gotten over the whole, Jason-has-a-girlfriend thing. I spent some more time with Crystal and Tara who seem really sympathetic. Even though they don't know that I like them, meaning the sympathy is in my head. Still, in my head, they're the best friends ever and are trying to help me get over it.

Today in gym, I'm asking Crystal what she wants for her birthday. She shrugs and says that she'll accept anything. "I'm honestly just excited to finally be a teenager. Wow! I can't believe how close I am!"

I smile. I'm not really jealous. She's had to wait just as long as I have to become a teenager. She just gets it first. "Wanna do our handshake?"

She nods and we high five, medium five, low five and complete the whole complicated process. Then we hunch over with laughter. Suddenly, Mimi and Tara approach. I never told you how lunch went. I'm sorry!

Mimi sat with us and basically didn't say anything to me. I felt very unwelcome. I glanced over at Ella a lot during the lunch. She didn't really pay too much attention to me, but I don't know why. Oh, who am I kidding? I know exactly why. Ella hates me now. I don't hate her. I actually feel really bad about what happened between us. I wish she would just listen to my apologies. She hasn't been listening to me at all. She's still giving me the silent treatment. I just wish I knew how to fix this. I would do it in an instant.

Anyway, back to gym class. Tara is basically talking about the big sleepover party she's holding.

Crystal is talking about us all coming over to celebrate her birthday. Mimi is talking about a "jerky" teacher that she has. I'm staring off into space, thinking about Ella. And Makayla too, but mostly Ella.

"What is wrong with you Liv?" Mimi asks. Oh, great. Tara taught her my "nickname" too. Everyone is going to call me Liv now, aren't they?

"Nothing," I answer, trying to avoid the whole my-best-friend-hates-me topic as much as possible. Mimi doesn't show any further interest, which is what I wanted to happen. Does Mimi ever show any further interest when it comes to me? Answer: No. No she does not. Mimi hates me. And I don't even know why.

Luckily, Crystal, queen of conversation, starts talking to her and she includes us all. How did any of this turn into my 7th grade life?

"Oh, guys, I heard you all in the chorus concert. You sounded really great. I'm so going into Chorus next year," she says. We all smile and thank her, but really, I'm still thinking about Ella. I can't help glancing at her and Makayla every now and then. They're talking happily and I see Makayla making weird hand motions. I roll my eyes. She's got my best friend completely fooled. She's probably glad that Ella hates me. I need to make up with Ella before this turns into something drastic. I may have forgotten to say that Makayla talks about me behind my back. If she says that I made my best friend hate me, then who knows what the social consequences could be for me.

"Liv!" Mimi snaps in my face. "Seriously, are you sick or something? What the heck is wrong with you today? You're usually the life of the party."

Me? The life of the party? Yeah right. It's never been "Olivia, life of the party." Always "Ella, life of the party" or "Crystal, life of the party".

I blush and say, "It's nothing. I'm just dealing with something right now. I don't want to talk about it." I catch her and Crystal exchanging a look but I don't know why. It kind of hurts my feelings. I'm not trying to make *anyone* hate me, but apparently, that's all I can do. Is that a talent? I can go into the talent show. Bring some people on stage and just make them hate me in record time. Or-

"Liv!" It's Tara now. "Wow, Mimi's right. You're really out of it today. Are you sure you don't want to go to the nurse? I can take you there."

I shake my head and try my best to keep up with the conversation in which I have absolutely nothing to contribute.

Chapter 4
A Normal Day in the Life of Me

I've accepted now that there are not going to be any more fun activities. School is in full session, teachers are ready to teach every morning no matter how much the kids really don't want it and everything is just class after class. So I think it'd be nice if I gave you a look at the normal day.

Block 1
Science

What we do in that class-This is pretty fun. I love my science teacher. She is really fun and nice, but it's hard in science class for me sometimes. I'm not really great at thinking like a scientist. But, usually we do experiments and then write about them. We have salmon because we are trying to save the. We're going to write about where to release them so that they have the opportunity to live the longest amount of time.

Friends in that class-The only friend I have in that class right now is Jason, but since classes are getting too big, some kids might be switched in. I doubt it though. Our science class is what Mrs. Keddman calls "The Perfect Size". At least I get to talk to Jason. I almost never do in other classes. Except I humiliate myself sometimes. Yeah, maybe I should stay away from talking to Jason. Anyway, I have one friend in that class.

Grade as of last trimester-My grade as of last quarter was an 89. Remember the whole final exam thing? Yeah, my grade still stayed an 89 after that. I mean, I guess I didn't really expect it to change, but I was kind of hoping. Somewhere. In the back of my mind. I really wanted it to change. But in the front of my mind, I knew that there was no way on earth that that could possibly change.

Block 2 and 3
ELA

What we do in that class-In ELA, we do exactly as it sounds. We do vocabulary worksheets, grammar worksheets, and read. Definitely the most fun class for me when we read but if we don't it's way too easy. Oh, and sometimes, we write. Usually it's informational pieces and boring argument paragraphs, but it's writing nonetheless. Plus, when she actually lets us do narratives, it makes me appreciate it even more. It's my favorite class by far. I mean, if you love to write as much as I do, it would be your favorite class too. Your all time favorite class by far!

Friends in that class-In this class, I have Tara, Jason and Mimi. Not that I'd exactly call Mimi a friend of mine, but I used to have Chloe and someone needs to take her place as my other friend. I can't just have one person like in science class. It's really uncomfortable every single day. It's nice that I have Tara. Before she came, I didn't have any close friends in that class, but Tara is a close friend, so I guess you could say that now I do have a close friend. If I didn't I would be really uncomfortable. That can't be ELA for me. It's my favorite class.

Grade as of last trimester-As of last quarter, my ELA grade was an average of a 97.5. I told you it's my favorite class. I've been reading since I was 4. It's pretty much my favorite thing to do besides write. Anyway, it's one of the highest grades I've ever gotten in my entire middle school career for something other than gym, art, or chorus where almost everyone gets a high grade because it's really not that hard to get a good grade in those classes. I was really, extraordinarily proud of myself for getting a great grade in that class.

Block 4
Chorus

What we do in that class-In Chorus, we sing. However, I don't really like a lot of the songs. Seriously, how can children possibly know these songs and get excited over them? I guess I can't complain too much though because the teacher is actually really nice to me and there are far worse classes than a class where we get to sing for 45 minutes. I bet you can agree with me on that.

Friends in that class-In this class, I have most of my friends. Ella, Jason, Tara, Ava, Katie, and...BRIANNA!!! I missed Brianna over the summer. She goes to camp (with Sierra) so when we got assigned different teams, I thought I'd never get to see her. I was wrong! I was so excited on the first day.

Grade as of last trimester-I got a 100. Not that it's really that difficult to get a hundred. As longs as you sing and don't talk, easy 100. There are some kids in there who really should be getting a 60 but are getting a hundred. Not sure I should be worried about this class bringing my GPA down too much. I mean, I don't think that I've ever gotten less than a 100 in this class. Well, actually, knock on wood that I've never gotten less than a 100 in this class. I don't want to jinx myself. That's the last thing that I need right now. Especially after that almost straight A's thing.

Block 5a
Lunch
Block 5b
Math

What we do in that class-Fractions, decimals, addition, subtraction, multiplication, division, integers, negatives-you name it! Math class has it all. Which is usually pretty cool. Math class is normal, but I like it because I guess I've always been at least a little talented. My mom is a math teacher so a lot of times, she works with me for a little while and helps me with whatever homework I don't understand. It's a benefit. Plus, a lot of kids ask me for help with their work because they call me the "math girl". Cool huh? I mean, I'm not sure that's fair. Is that a label? It sounds like a label. It's a good label-I'd rather have that then Stinky Face-but a label nonetheless.

Friends in that class-Jason. He's in every class, which makes every class an opportunity to embarrass myself. Sometimes I like to see him in every class. Other times it's weird to see him in every class. It's like...bye Jason. Oh, hey Jason. Didn't expect to see you there. Did

I mention that I like you? Because if I did, please forget that I ever said that. Ha ha ha. Yeah. That's the kind of thing that I have done to embarrass myself. Luckily I've never actually revealed that I like him before. Even I wasn't stupid enough to ever do that. I think you can agree that after knowing me for this long, that I have been pretty stupid in some parts so far this year. Also in that class, Crystal, which is a nice relief from embarrassing myself in front of Jason. A solid friend can do that I guess. Crystal is always there to save me when I'm being stupid. Which I almost always am when I'm not answering questions or doing worksheets. Why can't 7th grade be just like that? Where there is only one answer, and that's it. No second guessing. No worrying. One answer. No complications. That whole "no second guessing no worrying" thing is how I feel with Crystal. Because we are best friends.

Grade as of last trimester-95. A healthy middle between a 90 and 100 and a solid A. What I think is really sad is that I got the highest grade in all of class. I feel kind of bad for these people. (I only know it's the highest because based on how often every single person in this room needs my help and seeing the grades they get on tests when I have to help them revise it, there is no way that they are getting higher than a 95). Maybe, just maybe, Frederick, the second smartest kid in class-second to yours truly-got a 95, but that's the only person I think even had a shot at higher than an 80. Everyone else-sorry. I have to say, I'm not sure that you even passed math. Sorry. I just don't have too much faith in you. Oh well.

Block 6
History

What we do in that class-We read about things that have already happened from a big textbook. Yeah. Fun. Actually, though, I like history class. My teacher is nice and although it might not be my favorite subject, (to be honest it's not even remotely close) I still have an okay time. Besides, when it's history, I know that the day is almost over. I mean, it's 6th block and there is 8 blocks total. And the other two are fun blocks. I have a great time during history except for the actual part of sitting in a classroom and doing work. But that's not too bad either. Wait. Why didn't I think that history was fun again? Because I was totally wrong about that.

Friends in that class-Friend wise, this is my favorite class. I have Ella, Crystal, Jason, Tara and Ava. Katie was going to be in this class but because of High-C (That's a highly capable program for the really smart kids. I wanna be in High-C.) she got switched out. Now she's only in my gym class which really stinks sometimes but it's cool because I get to see her in lunch and gym. It's like a treat or something when I get to see her. Wait, that came out wrong.

Grade as of last trimester-A 96! That's the highest grade that I've ever gotten in history! I was so so so so excited to receive this grade. I could write an award speech or something. I would like to thank my teacher and all my best friends and my parents and my 10 year old brother George...the list could go on and on and on. Anyway, still really excited and thrilled! Woo hoo! Yeah! Awkward air fist bump! Kapow! Yeah...I'm not that popular...

Block 7a
French

What we do in that Class-We are learning french. Frenchy french french. It's really fun. I took it last year, and it's probably one of my favorite classes. Then again, all UA's except gym are my favorites. Anyway, French is actually pretty easy for me, because for some reason, I kind of am naturally talented. Last year, when we did get graded, I got a 99 for the trimester. That's pretty good I think. Some people don't even get grades that add up to that. I'm lucky to get that for the trimester. Anyway, I really like learning French because you never know when you'll need it, and plus, my teacher is really nice. French is one of the best classes ever.

Friends in that Class-I have all my friends in this class, which is nice. I get to see them all at once, but sometimes people get left out, which actually isn't great. I sit with them sometimes if they sit alone. No one deserves that. Well, except maybe Makayla. I could care less if Makayla is sitting alone, especially after the way she has been treating me all year. Which is like dirt. Which is the main reason I would happily let her sit alone if the opportunity came. Which so far it hasn't because everyone wants to sit next to Makayla. I don't understand it, but that's just how life is I guess. Life involves me getting hurt on a daily basis, not that I think Makayla getting hurt will make me feel any better.

Grade as of Last Trimester-We actually don't get graded, which is nice. It's kind of one less stress. I could always use one less stress. I mean, couldn't everyone use one less stress? I wish I didn't get graded in any of my classes. You know how much better that would be? To not be graded and not have to worry and just be able to be happy? It would be amazing, believe me. I would honestly love it, especially after last year's, "I almost got straight A's but not quite so I just need to keep on trying and eventually I might get it." Did you get any of that? It just means I don't want to get graded in any class because it would be easier and less stressful.

Block 7b
Art
What we do in that class-I think that you already know this, but in art class we do...get ready I'm going to blow your mind...art! Arts and crafts and all sorts of fun projects. I really like art class and it's even better because I have Crystal. Next year, when she joins chorus, I'm not really sure if that will happen but I'm just going to enjoy it. Anyway, I also like art class because my teacher is really nice and she's actually made a lot of money off of selling her paintings. If writing stories and books doesn't work out, maybe I'll become an artist. You know, maybe I will become an artist regardless. When this book is done, I can illustrate it. Yeah...I'm going to ponder that for a little bit longer. Instead of hiring someone, it would be easier to just do it myself. My decision is made!

Friends in that class-Just Crystal. But it's nice to get a little time away from everyone else. Crystal is really funny and nice and I like getting to spend an hour with her. I'm really lucky to have her as my friend. And maybe, just maybe, we can be best friends. That would be really nice. Not that I would ever ask her to be best friends. I learned that the hard way when I asked Bethany Harper to be my best friend in preschool before I met Ella and she said no. Ella must have seen me because the next day she walked up to me and asked me what my name is and all the normal making friends stuff and we were inseparable since then. It wasn't like that when I met Crystal in 1st grade. We just kind of said hello. We don't have to talk. It's weird. It was never like that with Ella, but maybe it doesn't have to be. This can be a new type of friendship.

Grade as of last trimester-100. Not that it's difficult. It's like Chorus. As long as you hand in your projects on time, you get a 100. It's supposed to be like that with gym too...you'll see where I'm going with that. Anyway, I think everyone in that class got a 100. I wasn't really expecting anything less. What would be cool is if they had 100+ for those really good kids. I would get a 100+. I always hand in my work early. Anyway, moving on to last block. Gym. My least favorite block by far. I think you've read the second chapter in September. You know how I feel about gym. If you haven't read it, go find a comfy place and read it.

Block 8
Gym

What we do in that class-Sports. Now, you've known me for a while I would say. Be honest now. Your honestly will only help me, I promise. I won't be mad. Now, do I sound like a sports person to you? Does Olivia Hamilton, master of falling on her face and embarrassing herself sound like a sports person to you? Yeah, didn't think so. Anyway, it's horrible in gym, but at least it's last block. I still despise gym though. Like on a scale of 1-10 it is a -10. That, my friend, is how much I really totally and completely hate gym.

Friends in that class-Crystal, Ella, Katie, Ava, Tara, Mimi, every other person who sits with us at lunch and every other person on my team. I don't think this one needs further explanations.

Grade as of last trimester-91. Now, normally all you'd need to do is change every day and you'd get a 100. But of course I have to get the toughest gym teacher ever. He says that I have to pass all these tests and stuff. I have no upper body strength! How am I supposed to do a pushup if I never learned and have no upper body strength?

Chapter 5
One Month into the Brand New Year

Woo hoo! 1 month down, 11 to go. About 4 months to go until I'm a teenager. 5 months to go until school ends. And my New Year's Resolution? It is to get Ella to not be mad at me anymore. Which I think will be my daily resolution until she finally forgives me.

Anyway, school has been okay. I don't love it, but by February, I don't think I've loved any school year, except maybe kindergarten and preschool. By first grade, I think I've accepted that school was not going to be all fun and games anymore. However, my teachers are all nice, and I have friends, so I guess I can't complain.

I still love SADD and Student Council, and whatever I do after school because it's fun. What I don't like is still the same thing that you can see on the previous page. Well, that's it. I guess I'll see you in February.

February

Chapter 1
I Finally Get my BFF Back

Ella still hasn't really talked to me, but I don't care. I've kinda stopped caring. I'm not sure. Maybe that's me becoming mature, now that I'm not really paying too much attention to what she's doing. That's what Crystal and Tara have been telling me to do for a while and I guess I'm finally listening to them. Anyways, at least they're my friends. I can count on that. Maybe they're the only best friends I still have. I know they're my best friends because I would do anything for them and I know they will do anything for me. Isn't that what friendship is supposed to be? Well, besides sleepovers and secrets that only they know. That's the friendship that Ella and I had. That's the friendship that I thought we always would have, no matter what happened to either of us, ever, we'd always still be best friends.

I can't wait for Valentine's Day. That's when I get to give everyone Valentine's. It's in about a week. When I make up with Ella, she's getting a Valentine, and Makayla is NOT! And, I can finally prove to Makayla that nothing can get in the way with me and Ella. Nothing can. Except, you know, this fight. But this is our first one ever. It is really impressive to me that we were able to go this long without having an argument, but it also makes this one extra hard to go through.

Anyway, to make that plan work, I have to make up with Ella now. I walk up to her in history. I hope she talks to me. If she doesn't, well, then, I don't know. At least I have Tara and Crystal. Not that either of them will compare, but they're really awesome. "Hey Els," I say shyly. I tuck a piece of hair behind my ear. I've never been unable to talk to her before. Is this what my friendship has turned into? My best friend hates me?

She looks at me and blinks as if to say, "Who me?" I feel horrible. My best friend doesn't think I'm talking to her. Or, maybe she knows and she just wants to hurt my feelings. She might be trying to make me feel like the enemy here. I can't let that happen, but in a way, I guess I am the enemy here. I made her upset. I made her hate me. I'm the one who didn't answer her last month. I'm the one who made her feel bad all the time. I am the enemy. And I couldn't be a worse one. I don't deserve to be her friend. She's too good for me.

I nod. She rolls her eyes. At least we still communicate solely with our eyes, even if it is to be annoyed at each other. I don't think anything, especially not a stupid fight, could ever come between that. Because right now, that eye communication is the most important thing to me. I think it's the only way that me and Ella are still together. Even if she hates me. Which she does. But I deserve it. I don't want it to be this way.

"Ella, you've gotta talk to me," I say, taking my assigned seat next to her. I recognize this as the conversation that we had when I was really mad at Ella last month. We pretty much said the same things. I know how it feels to be on this side of it. Take my word for it. It's horrible. I hate it. "Please. Just say one word. You're my best friend."

Ella sighs. "Fine. I'll talk. But you won't enjoy it. I was willing to apologize last month, but you didn't want to listen." I start to cut her off but she holds up her hands. Huh. I didn't know she was so forceful."Wait Olivia. Let me finish. I was really hurt. Suddenly, it's like you have all these new friends. I am really mad at you. This stupid conversation that I didn't even want to be in is over." She turns away. I can see her blinking. I didn't make her cry...did I? Did I make my best friend cry when she's already mad at me? I did. I'm a horrible person. I am the worst person who has ever lived. This is not looking good for me right now. I have to fix this right now. And I mean right now. You understand if you've ever made your best friend cry. It's the worst feeling in entire world to know that you've made someone who means the world to you cry. I'm going to fix this. I'm going to fix it now.

"Wait!" I sigh before Ella turns back around, icing me out until college. Don't say it won't happen. It totally could. "Ella, I'm so sorry. I never wanted to hurt your feelings. I kind of just acted in the moment and I was kind of in a bad mood when you tried to apologize. But you didn't have to do the whole two lunch table thing. That really hurt my feelings. I felt like you were laughing at me, and that hurt me badly." I look down at my desk. She thinks I'm lying. I know she does. Everything I've ever told her is the truth. She has to believe me! I don't know what I would do with myself if she didn't.

"I'm sorry too then," she says, looking at her lap. "I didn't mean to laugh at you. I would never laugh at you. I just felt like I had to do that to prove I had other friends." She looks at me and kinda half smiles, and I can see a glimpse of the old Ella in there. She's still there. She's not mad at me. She knows I would never hurt her on purpose. Welcome back, old Ella. I missed you. I missed my best friend.

"You do have other friends. You're like, the greatest person I know. You are extremely smart, all the teachers love you, you're outgoing, you're beautiful, you're funny, you're all around the most amazing just-turned-13-year old like EVER! That's why I love you so much. That's why we are all time BFF's. How could anyone not want to be your friend?" I ask. I do these crazy hand gestures to prove it. I think she thinks that I'm crazy and insane but I don't care, because I think she's known that for a while now.

"You'd be surprised," she mumbles. I don't believe her. I raise my eyebrows but ignore it. Now is not the time for arguing, even if I am trying to help her. Now is the time for apologizing. Now is the time for making her know that she is like the best person in the entire world for me. I'm not letting the opportunity pass me by again. I need to tell her exactly what I wanted to tell her last time but couldn't.

"Ella, I've loved you since we were 4 years old. Please don't let a stupid fight ruin 8 years of friendship." I smile at her, hoping I don't look as desperate as I feel. I probably do. To be honest, I don't care. She's my best friend and she should be able to see all sides of me, good and bad, crazy and sane, normal and desperate. Best friends - Olivia and Ella.

She smiles. "Thanks Olivia. I won't, I promise. I feel the same way." She holds out her arms for a hug and I accept it, a huge smile on my face. My best friend is back! I've waited for a month to get my best friend back. Now it's finally happening. I couldn't be happier.

"Now that that's done, wanna sleep over on Friday? We've got the dance and you could come over after." I ask. I'm still desperate, but know I know that she doesn't care. Because we're all back to normal. Best friends. Forever.

She nods and I smile as history class finally begins. I still don't notice Jason coming into class, but this time it's for a different reason. I'm sitting next to my best friend Ella who I'm never going to let get away from me again.

Chapter 2
Getting Picked

I like volunteering to do things in school. Seriously, I'll volunteer for anything. I probably have volunteered for everything. I want my name to be announced in front of the whole 7th grade, I want everyone to know me, I want to mean something to these people. I don't want to just be a face in the yearbook. I want to be someone who these people can say they saw on stage.

So, at every single assembly, I volunteer for whatever I can. Usually, Crystal or Ella give me weird looks and I just raise my hand higher. In fact, last year, I was so close to being chosen, but he went right past me. Ella and Crystal were right there. Crystal had smiled at me, trying not to laugh. I could see it in her eyes that she thought I was hilarious. I think she still does. I pouted and Ella actually did laugh a little bit. "Sorry Olivia," she said, rolling her eyes. I just shrugged, still keeping up the "I'm really upset" act. Ella had just paid attention to the assembly and I kept being all fake sad but really happy because I was just right there with Ella. We were together, and that's all that mattered. That's still all that matters.

I'm sitting at an assembly right now, missing advisory, which could possibly be the best part about this one. I really hate advisory, but I think you already know that based on how much I complain about it. There are two kids up on the stage right now. I didn't get picked again, not that I'm upset about it. I'm kind of used to it by now. I can be invisible at this school. Sometimes even my best friends don't realize when I'm there.

I'm bored out of my mind at this moment, not paying any attention to what any of these people are saying. I'm paying more attention to Eddie and Jerry, the boys on both sides of me, as they fight about who knows what. Eddie and Jerry are best friends so they are constantly fighting. I don't understand. I just got over a fight with my best friend, and Eddie and Jerry have them constantly? And they're still friends? Yeah. I don't understand boys' friendships either.

Anyway, the kids formally on the stage sit back down. Among them were Kim (Jason's girlfriend), TJ (no meaning to me), and Jessie (this really annoying girl in my advisory class). I could care less about them, but shift my attention back to the speaker.

"I'm going to need another volunteer," he's saying. Wait, what? I could volunteer. Totally! Definitely! What am I doing here, just thinking about volunteering? I raise my hand, then seeing Makayla with her hand up, raise it higher.

"The girl in green!" he says, pointing in my direction. I look down at my shirt. It's an aqua color with silver polka dots. Did he mean me? Was I actually picked for something? Or does he just see someone else with a green shirt and not see me there? I have no idea, but there's only one way to find out. I point to myself as if asking him and he nods. My heart starts racing and I run up to the stage. I got picked. I just can't believe it. It's still like a crazy thing to me.

"What's your name?" he asks me when I finally reach the top. Breathless, I take a second to look out at the crowd, but all I see is lights. Well, maybe that will make this a little bit easier. At least I don't have to feel like I'm talking to the entire 7th grade.

"Olivia Hamilton," I answer weakly. There are lights on me and I know everyone's looking. I feel this rush and, although I can't see much, I see Crystal and Ella both smiling really large. I know what they're happy that I was finally picked for something.

"Well, hello then, Olivia. How would you like to help me out?" he continues. I smile, and he takes that as a yes. "I just need you to look out into the audience and tell me how you feel." I nod. Not exactly what I pictured, but okay.

I look out, catching Crystal's eyes. She gives me a thumbs up. As my eyes adjust to the light, I see that everyone is looking at me with different facial expressions. Makayla looks like she's going to kill me later. Hopefully that's not actually going to happen. I might want to avoid Makayla for a little while. Ella looks proud and happy. My teachers look surprised that I would volunteer for something like this. Everyone else is pretty much giving me a blank stares. I smile weakly but no one smiles back. I look down as if saying, okay then. I feel like everyone and anyone who can possibly make fun of me is doing so.

"So, how do you feel?" the speaker asks me, snapping me out of a daze I didn't know I was in. I shrug.

"Overwhelmed. Terrified. Confused," I answer, hoping one of those is right. I have other words too, if he needs to hear them.

"All of those," he grins, looking impressed at my vocabulary, but I don't know why. Doesn't he know how a 12 year old girl talks?

I smile at them, showing all my teeth, including my braces, but no one reacts. OK then. Maybe I am invisible. On stage somehow I am invisible. What are the odds? Am I always invisible here, no matter what I do? I guess I am.

"Let's all give her a huge round of applause!" Wow. This is one energetic speaker. I'm not entirely sure why I came up here. Maybe I should have paid more attention. He may have been talking for a little while and I just wasn't paying attention to it. I try to look my best as everyone applauds. "Thank you very much Olivia." He shakes my hand and I smile towards him now. "You may go back to your seat now."

"Thank you," I answer. As I walk back to my seat, Crystal holds her hand out for a high-5 and it's not until I high-5 her that I realize how much I'm shaking. I'm shaking a lot. I'm still not over the fact that I actually got picked for something. I've been trying to get picked for something for as long as I can remember, so I can't believe that it actually happened.

We all have to leave in a few minutes, but actually, the rest of the day is not bad. The whole 7th grade knows me. I'm well known. And it terrifies me so much, but I volunteered and I got picked. I wouldn't be surprised if I was asked for autographs at lunch. Or I got to leave school early because there were people there from Hollywood and they want to invite me to go with them. Ok, it would be the most surprising thing that would have ever happened to me, but it's still something that I like imagining.

At lunch, Crystal and Tara both say that I did a great job. I wanted to ask what I did a "great job" on, but I don't want to sound like I'm fishing for compliments. I never want to be that girl. I don't like those kind of girls. But I feel like I'm becoming one of them. After that, the day is uneventful. Not that I was wishing for more congratulations but...I kinda was.

Don't hate me. I'm just like every other self conscious, insecure 12 year old girl out there.

An insecure, self conscious 12 year old someone who was picked to volunteer for something that was actually on stage.

Chapter 3
My Wonderful Friday

I wake up and already I'm feeling absolutely and positively sick. My stomach is killing me and my head is pounding, and in addition to me feeling like I'm going to be sick, my entire body is hurting me when I move. But I have a math test today, meaning I have to go to school. I force down some cereal and walk down the street to my bus stop, trying not to drag my feet.

"Hey Olivia!" Sierra says when she sees me. I put on a fake smile and walk over to her. "Excited it's Friday?"

I nod, faking enthusiasm for Sierra's sake. She doesn't need to know that I'm sick. "What about you? Got any plans for the weekend?"

She shakes her head, but I'm not really paying too much attention. My head is killing me, worse than before. We don't talk until we get on the bus. That's when...surprise...car sickness takes over my body and I feel like bleh. I just want to go to the nurse, but I know I have to wait until math is over at...1:15 pm. Math is over at 1:15 pm so I have to sit in school feeling sick until then. I mean, I guess I don't have to do the math test, but I studied really hard for it last night, and the last thing I need is to have to do it on Monday, when I will have forgotten everything I need to know. I can survive until then...can't I?

The first class I have is science. I like science, mostly because I get to see Jason and sit right next to him, but Jason's upset today. He doesn't seem like his normal self. "What's wrong?" I ask him, purely because I feel bad and have nothing else to say. Hey, I like the boy. I hate seeing him upset.

"Kim and I broke up." Jason says, a scowl still on his face. "Not that I care. The feeling was pretty mutual, I like someone else too. But she was *cheating* on me, Liv! Cheating!" He throws his hands up as if annoyed. I normally would correct him and say it's Olivia, but I'm not going to because the boy I like just called me Liv! It takes everything I have not to squeal. In fact, if I didn't feel so sick, I probably wouldn't have been able to control myself from squealing. The boy I like just called me Liv! Maybe that name's not so bad.

"I'm sorry Jason," I say, and an overwhelming headache comes on full force so I have to look away and stop talking.

Kim waltzes into class next, closely followed by Collin, her new boyfriend. It takes all my will not to scream at her. Wait. Did Jason say he likes someone else? Who is he close to in this class? Mayer. Yes! I have to ask Mayer who he has a crush on.

Mayer gives me nothing. I don't get to talk to him until right before chorus starts, but he doesn't reveal anything. Ugh. Chorus. I don't feel like singing.

I feel too horrible to notice that Crystal has switched into our class. "Olivia, is something wrong with you?" she asks. "You're usually much more lively than you are right now."

I do a half shrug. "I feel sick." My head is once again pounding and my car sickness feeling has gotten worse. How is that even possible? *I'M NOT IN A CAR!* I hold my head and try not to look mad, but I must.

I have to have a mad expression on my face because Crystal stops talking. I feel a little bad, but not enough to apologize. Instead, I take a deep breath and prepare to go into class. For the next hour, I have to put my sickness aside. I can deal with this for a little bit longer, I hope. At least if I get sick, I can go home. When I sit down in my normal seat, I say hi to Brianna, but don't tell her I'm sick because she would worry. Brianna worries about everything.

Finally, chorus is over. I have lunch and then math. I don't feel like eating right now. Tara, Crystal, and Mimi all talk nonstop, laughing and eating as usual, but I have nothing to contribute. Well, nothing except, I don't feel like talking to any of you, but I feel that would be rude. I put my head on the lunch table and just wait for the half hour to finally pass. When it does, I grab my lunch bag and head to my locker, getting ready to go to math, hopefully my last block.

The math test is probably the highlight of my day. I'm not sure if I did a great job, but I did the best I could considering how sick I feel right now. I can't really concentrate. It's kind of like when Jason talks to me. The test takes me a total of 20 minutes-it wasn't really hard at all, sick or not sick. I go to the nurse as soon as I'm done. She gives me a mint and an antacid and tells me to come see her if I don't get better. I thank her and take the "medicine", knowing it won't help and I won't be coming down. I'm not that desperate kid who needs to go home so badly and must continuously see the nurse. I'm pretty sure I can deal with this for a little bit longer.

I'm happy when history starts, but only because I know it's my last "real" class and my brain can relax when I'm done. Ella and Crystal exchange looks throughout the class, but I feel too bleh to say anything to them. I just half listen to the teacher as I imagine all the places that I would rather be right now. When the bell rings signaling French class, I'm relieved. As much as I love French, I already finished a lot of the work that other kids are just starting, so I know I can be in a quiet environment.

That's taken from me quickly. Everyone is talking in class because we have a substitute. I'm half involved in a game with me, Ella, Crystal, and Katie when Lexi screams across the room, "I know who you like now that you and Kim broke up, Jason!"

I feel my heart start to race at this, but I don't know why. Jason turns a light pink. "Who?" he smirks, thinking he has her. I should just stop listening right then. I already feel sick. I don't need to get hurt on top of that. I don't need to hear whatever Jason has to say. I am perfectly fine hoping he likes me but knowing he doesn't in the back of my head. But I need to listen. I apparently need to break my own heart. I need to hear what he has to say to Lexi about who he likes.

"You like Makayla!" Lexi smirks. Never have I been so mad. Of all people that Jason could have feelings for, it has to be the evil Makayla. Not me. It will never be me if he likes Makayla. Plus, I know for a fact that she likes Jason back. They'll probably start dating, since Makayla is prettier and smarter than me, even if I am nicer than she is.

I feel tears form in my eyes. It's not exactly heartbreak, but it feels like it's getting there. It's getting close to heartbreak. My stomach feels awful, like it's doing flips on a trampoline or something. My headache gets worse, it's like an intense pain all around my head. I feel like I'm going to be sick. Crystal sees me and asks to take me to the nurse. We walk down the hallway together and that's when I reveal everything. Everything from me liking Jason the moment I saw him walking down the hallway this past November on his first day here, to me and Ella's fight last month, to this morning feeling sick but only coming to school because of one stupid math test. Crystal listens sympathetically, and I know then that she's probably right up there in the Ella Anderson category of best friends. I wanted another Ella Anderson in my life, since the real one seems to have been falling short in my best friend world. Crystal has risen to the challenge and taken that top spot. She's a great friend.

The nurse takes my temperature, and declares that I have a fever. I go lie down in the back of the room on the cot as she calls whichever one of my parents will answer to come and pick me up. Perfect Friday.

Chapter 4
The One Thing that goes my Way

Guess who got all A's! Olivia got all A's! Who is a straight A student? Me! For the second trimester, I finally got straight A's, which has been my goal forever! It feels great!

I just don't know what my next goal is going to be. I got straight A's and finished the 2nd trimester of 7th grade, which has already been one of the most difficult times of my life. I run out to the buses at the end of the day and tell Ella and Crystal, who also got straight A's.

"Makayla got like all A+! She is super smart!" Ella says suddenly. It takes all I have not to roll my eyes. Now Ella is one-upping me, and it's not even really her. She's one-upping me with Makayla's stats. Speaking of Makayla, she approaches.

"Do I hear you bragging about me, Els?" she asks, pretending to be modest as she steals my nickname for Ella. Ella nods and scrunches up her nose, which tells me whatever's happening makes her happy. It must be some inside joke they have or something. They already have a bunch, and they're not great at hiding it from other people. I don't think they know how much it hurts me. Or maybe Makayla does and Ella is just too oblivious to see it.

"I was just telling them how smart you are," Ella says, smiling larger than she ever has with me. Makayla goes back to the pretend modest look.

"Well, yeah. I can also tutor. I actually tutor my boyfriend, Jason." Makayla smirks. I don't know how, but she knows I like him. She knew before I told Crystal. Maybe I look at him a certain way or something, but she knows. It makes me uncomfortable sometimes.

Anyway, Crystal looks at me sympathetically, but I don't react. This is why I didn't want to tell her. But I guess now that the secret's out, it's out, and Crystal is a really great friend. I know I can trust her with my secrets now.

I board the bus with my smile fading but still there. "Hey Sierra!" I greet my friend. "How was school? Good? Yeah, well, I got my report card!"

"All A's?" she asks. I nod vigorously and we squeal. She's not jealous, I know she's not, because she's always been an amazing student.

We talk the whole way home, and when we get off the bus, I walk with her to her house. It only takes about 30 seconds, so afterwards I walk back to my own house as I listen to music from my phone. Neither of my parents are there yet, so I greet Peanut and call my mom. I don't tell her about my straight A's. That's not really something I can tell somebody over the phone. She says she should be home in about an hour. When she finally gets home, I show her my report card, my straight A's!

Chapter 5
FINALLY!

Now that the trimester is officially over, I'm more than halfway done with 7th grade, which is really awesome. I'm more than halfway done with one of the weirdest years of my life. Now, there is some interesting stuff coming up. We have a field trip that's actually overnight. My birthday is this trimester. I'm really excited to see where the last part of the year takes me. Hopefully it's not smack dab into more Makayla drama. Not that that wouldn't be totally *awesome!* Because I love Makayla drama - any type of drama! Yep. Sarcasm.

I can't help but be happy though. I mean, the second trimester is done. I won't have to worry too much now, because this is when we will have some field trips and the rest of the year will be easier knowing that the teachers all know and hopefully like me. I know what 7th grade is like now. I have a strong idea of what 8th grade will be like. There is no need to worry, because I know what I need to know.

We have the weekend off now, and there's no homework, so Tara, Crystal and I will hang out a lot. They're sleeping over on Saturday night to celebrate my all A's. I couldn't be happier.

March

Chapter 1
Dalton Gommes-Part 1

These two chapters are probably going to be the longest ones in the book. Just warning you ahead of time.

We are in school on the first day of March. "On Friday," Mr. Lion says, "We will be going on our first overnight field trip. Please return these permission slips."

He hands these out and Jason whispers, "You think you're going Liv?"

Eep! He called me Liv! I shouldn't embarrass myself. He thinks I'm cool! Or maybe he thought I liked to be called Liv...I'm going with the first one. I smile. "It's likely. I mean, yes. I mean, I have to ask. I mean..." I avoid eye contact. OK, I need lessons.

"Me too," he says and stops talking to me. I mentally face palm myself.

My parents agree it's a good idea and on Friday, we're all at the school at 6:30 am. Literally everyone at our lunch table, including me, is in one cabin. We are all excited but exhausted. Tara had decided not to go and Mimi got put in another cabin, so I talk to Crystal. It's nice to talk to her one on one. "Excited?" I ask.

"Mostly," she says. "OK, a lot. Our first overnight! I bet it's going to be awesome!" I nod excitedly and our attention is turned to Mrs. Jack, who has started to speak. She tells us all about the trip! And I have to work really hard to contain my squealing. OUR FIRST OVERNIGHT!

At 7 am, we all board the buses. I sit next to Crystal and put our suitcases in the next seat over. Since it's about a half hour away, the bus driver puts on music. For me and Crystal, the bus ride is a dance party filled with laughing, talking and of course, dancing.

When the music dies down, the bus is still noisy. "So, have you talked to Jason lately?" Crystal asks me, wiggling her eyebrows. I blush.

"This is why I didn't want to tell you my feelings. No. And honestly, I embarrass myself literally whenever I talk to him. I don't know what to say. Maybe it's best if I don't talk to him. You know, at all," I look down. Maybe it's not Jason. Maybe it has nothing to do with Jason at all. Maybe I just can't talk to people. At least I know Crystal will be my friend no matter what I say. Unlike Jason who will probably only like me if I'm cool around him all the time.

Crystal shrugs and the bus pulls into Dalton Gommes. Every single 7th grader cheers and Crystal and

I cover our ears, giggling. It's still super exciting. Everyone thinks so. The teachers tell us to get off the bus in an orderly fashion. Yeah right. You have a better chance of telling a wild lion not to attack someone poking him with a stick. Okay, that made no sense. Let's go with a classic. You have a better chance of being struck by lightning.

We find our cabins pretty much as soon as we get off the bus. Our cabin is the best. It has a TV. The teachers said not to use it. We all agreed yesterday not to. Why would we purposely go against the teachers? Don't we want them to trust us? We have them all next year too.

Anyway, the rooms in our cabin are better than the others. There are bunk beds in each room. In one room, there are two sets of bunk beds. Crystal and I take one room, Makayla and Ella are in another, and Katie, Lisa, Jenny, and Ava are in the one with two sets. We can't stay in the cabin for too long. We've got to get out and start doing some activities.

The first thing we do is find out our groups. I thought it would just be our cabins, but as Ella and I are split up, I realize I thought wrong. Wow. It seems like everyone has been split up so far. There are two groups left to be put in, and it's me, Crystal, Katie, and Lisa who still have to be put into a group. As the last person's name is called, Jerry Marcer, the four of us breathe sighs of relief. We won't have to be split up.

Our group leader, Terry, is nice. She seems to have a sense of humor, and since we are the only girls, tends to talk with us more so than the boys. I like my group. It has 3 of my friends, Jason, and three other boys: Aaron, Chance, and Sam. I don't know them that well, but they've never been a problem for me.

The girls tend to stay together and the boys mess around when we go for the hike. Everyone has warm coats on, except me of course. I chose to bring a sweatshirt. I can't complain that I'm cold though because Katie, Lisa, and the boys don't need to know and Crystal can tell.

Anyway, after a hike my feet are killing me, and it's not even 10:00 am yet! I didn't bring sneakers because the ground is covered in snow, but now I'm kinda wishing I had. Maybe I wouldn't be freezing right now because my feet somehow got covered in snow anyway.

Luckily, the next thing we do is inside. We play this weird, yet super fun, game. At the end, Crystal and I are laughing really hard. We've already decided to just have fun this trip. Or at least I have. So far, this is like a two day long gym class for me. Not really one of my strengths, but I try to have fun. I don't win, and neither do any of the girls for that matter. The winner is Aaron, who is super athletic, more so than I thought.

They let us talk and warm up for a little while after that, which is nice, but I can't help wondering how Ella's doing. I'm worried about her, considering the fact that she's a little shy. Just a little. OK, a lot shy. But she's still my best friend, and I wouldn't trade that fact for the world plus a million dollars.

As we finally start to warm up, we have to go back outside. We've got about a half hour before we can warm up again for lunch at 11:45 am. We hike again, but now it's more fun because we're not freezing. So, in conclusion, it's kind of fun but, it's still hiking.

FINALLY! FINALLY! FINALLY! Lunch time! I am starving. I haven't eaten since breakfast about 6 hours ago. They have a ton of different types of food, and I take a little bit of everything, along with Crystal, then we sit down at our assigned table. Turns out we have to sit with our groups. I notice Ella is talking to someone in her group, and I'm glad she found someone to talk to. I talk to Crystal, Katie, and Lisa. We also talk to Terry.

Lunch is over way too quickly, and they let us play outside. "Ella!" I say, running over to her dramatically. "I missed you." I wipe a fake tear. Ella giggles. I smile. I like knowing that I made her laugh

"Me too," she says. "How's your group?"

"Fun, but I miss you. It's weird not sitting next to you in lunch." This hasn't happened since kindergarten, and that's because we didn't eat lunch at school. But even then, sometimes Ella came over my house or vice-versa after school. We'd just eat lunch together then. So yeah, it's very weird to not have her right next to me at lunch.

"Hey Olivia," Makayla says, all fake nice. "Do you mind if me and Ella talk for a little while?"

I look at Ella. She gives me a questioning look, oblivious to what's going on. I shrug, not knowing what else to say, and walk away. I join Crystal, Katie, Jenny, Lisa, and Ava over in the deeper part of the snow.

5 minutes - Not enough time to do anything. At least we've got cabin time in an hour. Crystal, Lisa, Katie and I link arms and walk out of the field as we reunite with our group. As we hike, Terry tells us all the schedule for today. We'll be hiking until 3:00 pm, then we'll have an hour of cabin time. At 4 pm, we'll play another game, and we'll eat at 5:30 pm. At 6:30 pm, we'll go on "The Underground Railroad", which will be about 2 hours. I'm not sure I could last 10 minutes, but oh well. Anyway, at 8:30 pm we go back to the cabin, and can hang out for a while. Lights out at 11. I'm pretty worried that I won't be able to sleep. What happens then? Do I just sit there in my bed all night waiting for the morning to come? I hope not. Because with my luck, that's exactly what will end up happening to me, because I'm me.

I talk to Crystal for most of the walk. Ok, my feet are *killing* me. How did slaves go across the Underground Railroad? How did immigrants come all the way to America in the "olden days"? This is just a hike. I can barely walk a hike. Well, my self-esteem has been badly bruised.

As the hike comes to an end, and we finally have cabin time, I collapse on the bed. I am exhausted. "Olivia!" I hear Ava call from the largest room. "We're playing Guess! Wanna play?"

"Yeah, sure!" I yell out, and run over. Mrs. Keller is in there, which makes me slightly uncomfortable. It goes away quickly though, because Jenny puts a blue plastic headband with a mysterious card on it on my head. I have no idea what it says. I guess that's the point of the game. I've never played it before, except once when I was 7 with George. I don't think we even played by the rules. We both cheated. Turns out, Guess is an easy game. You aren't allowed to see what your card says, and using clues that the audience gives you and asking questions. If you figure it out, you get a new card. We continue playing and laugh as Mrs. Keller gives us different clues. Suddenly, someone knocks on the door, telling us we've got 5 minutes before Cabin Time is over. We put the game away and walk out together.

As we join together in our groups, I find myself right near Jason. "Hey Liv!" he says excitedly. "Having fun?"

"Yeah, I guess so. I mean, I just had cabin time. And you did too. And I think all the groups did. Was your cabin time enjoyable? Because mine was. Wait. I think I said that already." I blush and force myself to stop talking.

"Okay.." he says. "Yeah, mine was pretty fun. We played Guess and-"

"WE DID TOO!" I interrupt him, throwing my hands up in the air. Suddenly, I realize how loud that was and clear my throat. "Um, yeah. We also played Guess."

Jason laughs and I turn a brighter red than ever before. "Yeah, well, it's fun." As we realize Terry is talking to us, we stop talking.

Crystal looks like she's trying to hold in a giggle. She had to have listened to the conversation. "You could have helped me," I say as we walk inside to the game room. Crystal shrugs and still looks like she's trying not to giggle.

"You seriously need lessons, Liv." I smirk at her.

"Please don't call me Liv!" I say, but she can tell I'm really half kidding. She knows I've just accepted Liv as my nickname by now. Which is okay I guess, but I kind of miss the days where I wasn't nicknamed Liv and I was just Olivia.

The day is mostly uneventful after this, at least until the underground railroad. It's dark and we walk out with our groups. I smile as I talk with Crystal, Lisa and Katie. At one point though, there is a hole. I don't see it because of the darkness. Lisa and Katie keep walking when I fall in, but Crystal realizes I'm not there almost immediately.

I twisted my knee. This is one of the most painful things ever. If twisting it feels like this, I don't want to see what it's like when it's broken. It feels like I'm being shot in the knee repeatedly. There is throbbing pain and I don't want to talk. It feels like what happened to my ankle in July. Except, I was at my house and I was just running around in the backyard. Now, I'm here, my parents are in my house, and none of them probably just twisted their knee and feel like they are going to die or faint from the pain. I'm all alone. That makes me a little bit nervous. I'm moving around in the hole because of the pain. I try so hard to hold in the tears, and I blink them back eventually. Crystal, of course, comes over to me which makes me happy. At least she's with me.

"Olivia! Are you okay?" Crystal asks, kneeling by me. I nod, tears forming in my eyes again. No. I will not cry in front of the group. If I do, then they'll think of me as a crybaby. "C'mon," Crystal says, grabbing my hand and helping me up. She supports me by putting her arm under my arm so I don't fall over. I thank her, and all of a sudden the tears come out.

"I'm so sorry," I say as I stand up. Crystal tells me it's okay and I'm still crying. Way to not be a crybaby. I'm pretty much sobbing.

After the underground railroad, all I want to do is sleep, so we end up going to bed at around 10:30 pm. It's been a long day and I'm asleep almost immediately.

Chapter 2
Dalton Gommes-Part 2

I'm not sure what time it is when I wake up, but I do know I'm the first one. My knee doesn't hurt me as badly as it did last night, so I get up, walk to the kitchen and look at the time. The clock is on the stove. This cabin is like a little house. It's adorable! Anyway, back to the time when I wake up: 6:02 am. Great.

I go back to my own room, knowing I won't be able to go back to sleep, and write a random story that I started a little while ago in my notebook for a little while, until everyone else wakes up. It's not a whole lot later. I don't think anyone is able to sleep so well in these beds. They are kind of like rocks. But at least the field trip itself is really fun and awesome.

Katie is first. I see her get up to check the time and I run over to her. "Hey Katie!" I say. "How'd you sleep?" I'm bouncing and Katie raises her eyebrows. I don't care. She's not judging me. Katie is one of my friends, and my real friends don't judge me.

Katie, ignoring my question says, "Wow. You're hyper for 6:30 am in the morning." I shrug and she shakes her head, as if questioning how the heck I'm so awake. The truth is, after being awake for a half hour, I am bored out of my mind and desperate for someone to talk to.

After that, everyone slowly wakes up. Ava's next, then Crystal, then Ella, then Lisa, then Jenny and Makayla walk out of their rooms at the same time. When everyone is awake, the clock says 8:49 am, which is good, because the first activity is at 9:00 am. We all rush to get dressed and brush our hair and teeth, which is not easy in a cabin of 9 girls. We finish and run out the door just as the bell signals activities starting.

We are told to join our field groups. Not a problem. Lisa, Crystal and I are talking when Jason walks up to us and says "I just got a new girlfriend!"

"That's great!" Lisa says, oblivious to my feelings. It's like a punch in the gut. Crystal gives Jason a smile and looks at me with a face that says, *Are you okay?*

I nod. Biggest lie I've ever told. Or, biggest lie I've ever implied I guess, since I didn't actually tell Crystal that I was okay officially. All I did was nod.

"So, who is it?" I ask, hoping my smile doesn't look too fake. I'm not sure how well that's working out for me. I'm pretty sure that I have the fakest looking smile in all of Dalton Gommes so I wouldn't be surprised. Notice how when I'm not worried about him liking me back I can talk normally around him.

"It's Makayla. She's beautiful, popular, and super cool," Jason says. Jason, of course would date Makayla. It takes everything I have to not roll my eyes. "We're not really doing anything, but..."

I nod and smile. "You guys have fun." Then I turn away, trying to hold back my tears, again. It's amazing how many times I'm ready to cry in not even 15 hours.

Anyway, we start playing a game, I have not idea what it's called, but the whole time, all I can think about is the two of them together. I decide to talk to Jason again at breakfast, and maybe things will go back to normal. Breakfast is at 9:30 am. It's 9:05 am. I can wait. Breakfast time finally comes. After pancakes (that don't taste frozen), I ask Jason how his cabin is.

"It's cool. How's yours?" He asks.

He cares. He cares about how my life is! He could like me! Or maybe it's just because I asked him and he wants to be polite. I'm going with the first one. "Nice," I squeak out. At least I can use normal words around him now. And, you know, squeak like a true human being. How is it that I still need lessons? He likes someone else! Move on Olivia! Move on!

Jason nods and starts talking to one of the boys. I turn to Crystal. "Better?" Crystal shakes her head and I pout. We join Ella's group for the next activity. "Hey Els!" I shout, running over to her. She starts running over to me too.

"I'm so glad we have this activity together," she says.

"Yeah me too. But at least I have friends. I feel worse for you," I answer. She shrugs and I can tell she isn't really going to be honest with me, no matter what she says next.

"You don't need to feel bad for me. Well, not worse than with you. I'm fine, I promise," she continues, touching my shoulder as we talk. Our talking is interrupted when we start the hike, but halfway through, we're allowed to talk again.

"Enjoying your field group?" I ask.

"Not too much. We can't even eat lunch together. How unfair is that?" she answers me. I just shrug. She's not really asking for answers right now.

"I can't wait until we can just eat lunch in school again. No drama, well except I sit with Tara, Crystal, and Mimi now. But I still kinda sit next to you," I say, trying to make her feel better. I don't think it works. She looks almost depressed.

"Yeah. Um, about that. I miss sitting next to you Olivia. But I can't anymore. Makayla and I are going to sit with Liera on Monday. I hope you don't mind..." Ella looks at the snow, but I decide my best bet is to just lie for the second time today. So far, it's helped out Crystal feel better and not feel bad for me, and now it will help Ella feel better and not feel bad for me. It's the perfect compromise. Well, for everyone else.

"Yeah. That's fine. Go ahead. Sit where you want. It's not like there are assigned tables or anything. I have to learn to share you." I include the last part as a joke, but there's awkwardness in the air now. How did this happen? We used to be able to talk for hours on end. Once, when we were 8, we played a game of Would You Rather all night, and it was all the hard ones because we knew each other's secrets. What's happening with us?

Awkward silence. Crystal joins us and raises her eyebrows. "Olivia Hamilton and Ella Anderson not talking? This is a first." "Hey Crystal," I say. I want to hug her, but that might make Ella feel bad so I don't. We just keep hiking in uncomfortable silence.

The hike lasts until 11:45 am, which means it's an hour and 15 minutes. Which means we have 15 minutes before lunch starts to warm up. In the rec room, all the groups are there, and Ella joins Makayla. Everyone else from our lunch table plays truth or dare.

"OK, Olivia, truth or dare?" Ava asks me.

"Truth," I answer. I am horrible at dares. Better to just answer a question.

"Who do you like?" Ava asks.

"Umm...do I have to answer?" I ask, squirming in my seat.

Everyone nods, and Crystal says, "Olivia, it's not that big of a deal. You're fine."

"OK, OK. I um...yeah so..." I can't tell them. Not now. Not when he has a girlfriend.The bell rings and I jump up, hoping they'll forget. "That's the bell, oh darn, ok let's go to lunch." Everyone rolls their eyes but heads out.

At lunch, luckily, no one brings up the question. We all just talk and eat like normal, and I manage to make it a whole lunch without being creepy and awkward around Jason. I know. It's a first for me. Anyway, as lunch ends and recreation time begins, everyone crowds around to see something, I don't know what. When I finally see it, I'm shocked.

Jason and Makayla are holding hands in public not caring who sees them. My blood is boiling. I can't do anything about it. I want to throw up!

"C'mon Olivia. Let's go over here," Crystal says, dragging me away from the scene of the crime. I nod and walk over with her.

"I didn't realize that they were actually dating. I thought that Jason just liked Makayla, and as mad as I was, it would be better than them dating. I didn't think that they would start dating each other," I say, trying not to cry.

"I know," Crystal says. "It really stinks."

I don't think Crystal knows what I'm going through. No one's ever mean to her. The guy she likes likes her back. She is pretty, popular, and sometimes I feel like she includes me because she feels bad for me because Tara and Mimi are pretty popular.

I shrug and stay silent. I don't really feel like talking. Recreation time ends, but I'm silent for about an hour. At 2:30 pm , Jason finally asks me what's wrong.

"Well, nothing," I say. "Nothing is wrong. But I have a question."

"Go ahead, Liv."

I blush and say, "Hypothetically speaking, what if a girl liked someone, but he had another girlfriend. How should that girl react?"

Jason looks like he's thinking. Finally, he says, "Well, I'm not going to push it to see who you like. Secondly, I don't think you should make a big deal out of it. This guy probably won't be with this girl forever. Don't worry." Then he turns and starts talking to Aaron before I can thank him. I nod. I'm not going to start obsessing about this. Jason is right. I'm glad he decided not to push it. He's a good friend. This is why I like him.

Soon, it's 3:00 pm with one more hour until we leave. I'm going to miss this place. As I look around at the cabin one last time, (we're all packed up) I smile and follow them out. We all hang out as one big group for the last hour and as 4:00 pm rolls around, we all say goodbye and board the buses. The group leaders are waving goodbye to us.

I sit next to Crystal on the bus again, but this time it's quieter. No one's as excited, but we still talk. I mean, the magic and anticipation of not knowing what will happen is gone. Why would anyone be extremely excited for this? Answer, they wouldn't be. It's over. Eventually, we pull into the school. My mom and George are waiting there and I tell them all about my adventure. My biggest adventure yet, just like that, gone.

Chapter 3

The Diamond

A few weeks have passed since Dalton Gommes. Makayla and Jason are still dating (ugh) and I have just been hanging out with all my new non-betraying friends.

One day, my friends beg me to go out for recess. "Liv, please come outside with us," Tara pleads.

"Yeah, please. Recess is only 5 minutes," Mimi continues. I finally give in and go out. When I realize Ella, Makayla, Katie, Ava, Jenny, and Lisa are outside as well, I automatically regret my decision.

It starts out okay. I mean, I am not a fan of recess as it is, and since we've only got 5 minutes, I mostly just talk to my friends and Makayla. At one point, she gets up, makes a diamond in the thinning snow, and says, "Don't step in this diamond." Well, no. She doesn't calmly say it. It's a command and she's looking directly at me when she says it. I just shrug in return. I don't need more drama. I've got enough for a lifetime.

Anyway, the whistle blows. I'm still trying to avoid stepping on the stupid diamond, but I'm going to be late. It's a diamond in the already melting snow, and the 5th graders will no doubt step on it. So, I give up on trying to find a way out of it and step on the diamond.

Everything seems okay. I don't think Makayla noticed, but now I realize I'm wrong. She approaches me in class before the teacher comes in. "Olivia," she asks. All that's going through my mind is "Why is she talking to me? She's been not talking to me and I've been fine with that. Why is she talking to me?"

"Why did you step on that diamond in the snow when I politely asked you not to?" she asks, a fake sweetness in her voice. Instead of helping me out, all the kids just stand there. I have to take matters into my own hands. I stand up and take a deep breath.

"How was I supposed to *avoid* stepping on that diamond? It wasn't exactly in the most convenient spot," I say, hoping my voice isn't as shaky as it sounds in my head. I need to sound confident. When I look at her face, I can tell she doesn't know what I mean. Okay, I guess that did sound a little nerdy. Maybe I should repeat that. No. She doesn't deserve it. Let her be confused. I keep going. "And besides Makayla, all I did is step on your stupid diamond. You've done much worse to me. You know exactly what you've done."

Makayla looks shocked that I was ready with a comeback. I stand confidently as she walks back to her seat. I sit back down, and Crystal walks over.

"Um, Olivia, I saw the end of that and I have one question. What the heck happened?" she asks, looking generally confused, as does the rest of the class. I tell Crystal everything. "And I needed to say that. She was trying to make me feel stupid in front of the class."

Crystal nods. "Great job Olivia!" We high-5 and I actually feel good for about 2 seconds. Then, I'm terrified. I just stood up to Makayla. And I won! What happens now? Does she try to get revenge. Needless to say, I'm having a lot of trouble focusing in class today.

The rest of the day drags on. I'm determined to avoid Makayla at all costs. When we're finally ready to board the buses, she comes up to me at my locker. "You're just a little meanie!"

Even though it sounds stupid, I laugh. "Meanie? The best you could come up with is meanie? Sorry Makayla, I've got a bus to catch." I sling my backpack over my shoulder and catch up with Crystal so we can walk out together. I'm not terrified anymore. Now I'm just happy.

Chapter 4

The Meeting...

It's funny. When you think that the worst thing just happens, another thing comes along and makes it that much worse.

This is a Washington DC meeting. It doesn't seem like it'd be that bad, does it? It's during advisory, the trip is next year. What's not to love?

Answer: Everything. The fact that it's during advisory makes it horrible. I'm stuck between two kids who won't stop talking. I have to keep asking them and then they call me a dork and a weirdo and a nerd, and I can't take it. I keep wishing for one friend, at least, in my class.

As I sit, only half listening to the speaker, who is really just Mrs. Jack, I keep thinking about how cool is it that we get to go to Washington DC next April. Then, as time drags on, I decide to stop paying attention entirely. Well, not to the meeting. That has some important stuff in it. I stop paying attention to things that are just unimportant such as what's going on in my head and the two boys that are now playing Rock Paper Scissors on opposite sides of me.

Mrs. Jack keeps on talking, and I try to listen, but with the boys next to me, arguing about who knows what, that's pretty hard to do. Even though I can't hear her very well, I can't wait for Washington DC.

Chapter 5
Almost Over

Wow. I can't believe 7th grade is almost over. It's the end of March and now I've got 8th grade and everything else. I can't wait to see where the rest of the year takes me. It's going to be so great and possibly the most stressful, but also the best. I'm going to be 13 soon. That's a teenager. Teenage years are going to be amazing. They may be a little stressful, but now, what part of my life won't be? I'm growing up!

April

Chapter 1
The Application

In the teacher's opinion's, school is wrapping up. They're getting us ready for the next year, and the 8th graders are ready to go to high school. I'm ready to be the oldest in the school, but before 8th grade starts, they have to pick all the "highly capable" students. I want to be one of them. Applications must be sent in.

I have to apply to be highly capable. If I don't get in, like in 5th grade, they are telling me that I'm not as highly capable as I thought I was. That's not a self-esteem booster.

"If you would like to be in High-C this upcoming year, these applications must be handed in as soon as possible," Mrs. Jack is saying. She hands them out to everyone and I look it over. Alright, so far so good. I have to write a paragraph which is looking positive. I like writing. That's my strong point. At least I hope so.

I take the paper home and put it on the counter so my parents can look it over. It probably won't be too much of a problem. I've wanted to do this since I was 8 years old. Someone kept leaving my class, and I was like, "What are they doing?" Later in the year, I found out that they were doing an extra project. I thought that would be so awesome and cool. After trying to get in for almost 5 years, this is my last try.

My parents say it's fine if I do it, so I sit down at the computer to write my paragraph. What makes me qualified to be in High-C? I could say that I got good grades, but they can just look at my report card to see that. I could say that I'd work hard, but who knows how many other kids say that? No, I need something that is going to separate me from everyone else who is applying. After dinner, I still have nothing.

"What are you doing Olivia?" George asks me at about 7:30.

"I'm writing this essay thing. Or trying to. It's not exactly working out," I say. I'm frustrated, I'll admit it. I never thought it would be so difficult to write something. I've never had this much trouble before. I just have to think really hard. Just think about why I would be a good High-C participant.

About 2 hours pass and I'm staring at the white piece of paper on my docs account. It's almost 10 o'clock and I really would just like to go to bed, but I still have absolutely nothing written down. What am I supposed to write. Let's start with my name. I write out a rough draft on a piece of paper with my hand. I'll edit it after.

My name is Olivia Hamilton and I am in 7th grade.

Perfect! Perfect perfect perfect perfect absolutely *perfect!* I type this out. It takes a little more thinking, but once I get past the introduction, the words flow to me like whenever I start writing. Before I know it, I'm finishing up with the sentence, *I really hope you pick me to be in the highly capable program*, and I'm getting ready to print it out.

That was surprisingly easy. They say that they are going to try to alert me as soon as possible. I really hope it's soon. I can hand in the application tomorrow and maybe whoever runs it will see that I do things on time and I will be a perfect addition to the High-C program.

Woo! I am so going to nail this!

7th grade. Easy as pie. Or you know, much much harder than pie.

Chapter 2
KWN! (Not as awesome as it sounds)

I may have forgotten to include a small portion in this book. The fact that we have to watch this news program that talks about current events in the world. I hate it. I hate it so much!!!

It's not horrible. I should be fair and make that fair right now. It's just the events scare me. For example, the host is nice, but he tends to talk about deaths by this new sickness I've never heard of or a natural disaster that I didn't even know existed. Some parts are funny and talk about animals, but most parts do not. Get it now? Anyway, I haven't brought it up because I don't want to seem like I hate everything about school. But, today it's awful.

I'm sitting in history class right now, talking to Ella and Crystal. I'm not supposed to watch it in Social Studies. It's a Tuesday. On Tuesdays, we watch Kids World News (KWN) in math class. At least Mr. Lion lets me read while it's on. I'm not sure Mrs. Jack would let me. So when the theme music starts playing, I want to scream, "No! No, Tuesday's the only day that I'm safe from KWN! Today is Tuesday!" I keep my mouth shut and look at the screen, knowing it's my only option. I already know it's bad the second he starts talking.

First, it's the normal stuff. Turns out, humans can get the plague. All that has to happen is getting bit by an infected flea. And guess what? That's impossible to avoid. You've gotta have a ton of bug spray. A ton. Like, from now on, bug spray is my cologne. Or my perfume, since girls don't generally wear cologne.

Anyway, another thing that he talks about today is the fact that a lot of oceans are infected with diseases. I don't even know what half of them are. How am I supposed to avoid them if I don't even know what they are? That can turn out to be a huge problem in my life, so there goes the fun times I wanted to have at the beach this summer, unless it gets fixed before that. The rest of the show drags on, but I think you get the picture.

As it is finally over, I smile. I don't want people to think I hate this show, but I do. Ella looks at me, like "What's wrong with you?" I shrug. I just think she doesn't pay attention to me when KWN ends, because this is actually normal for me.

I see Jason in the hallway. He seems upset about something. "Hey Jason. What's up?" I ask, not even taking into account that I'm not stuttering or embarrassing myself. Maybe Makayla broke up with him. Oh, how great would that be? Well, not that Jason would be all upset, but Makayla and Jason wouldn't be dating anymore.

"Oh nothing. Just the normal, you know, Makayla just broke up with me during KWN because she says I spend too much time in the ocean and she's scared that I have this stupid disease that you can apparently get. We just had math. I had no idea she was so shallow. I thought she was someone different. I guess I was wrong," Jason says, rolling his eyes.

Yeah, I thought she would be different too. But she's still same old meanie Makayla, and it's better you realize that sooner or later Jason. It's better for all of us. I promise, I think, nodding at him. I sigh sympathetically, but inside, I couldn't be happier.

Well, not that I want Makayla to be miserable, but it's nice that I don't have to watch her anymore dating the guy that I have a crush on. This is going to be nice. Maybe Makayla's really upset right now. Oh, how great would that be? She would be so upset and Ella, who's never had a crush on a boy, wouldn't know how to handle it. Maybe KWN's not so bad after all. Scratch that. It's still pretty bad.

Chapter 3
Life as we know it

Have you ever felt like the entire life you thought you knew just disappeared beneath you? That's how I feel right now. Makayla is talking about me in her art club. I don't know why. I'm sitting in there, since that Crystal and I decided to join. We are kind of isolated and no one, and I mean *no one,* is talking to us. Crystal's looking at me with a look of confusion. I don't know what's going on. I look over, looking for a friendly face. Everyone's talking and Makayla is shooting me dirty looks. Everyone is shooting me dirty looks!.

I finally see a quiet girl who has to be in 5th grade. She keeps looking at me, her brown eyes large and pleading as she draws a picture by herself. I give Crystal the "one second" sign and walk over to her.

"Hey. I'm Olivia," I say to her.

"I know who you are. Everyone does. But, hi. I'm Quinn," the girl says. She has a quiet voice and she reminds me of a younger me.

"Wait, how does everyone know who I am?" I ask.

"You're like, infamous in here. Makayla always says that you say you hate everything about her. Everyone knows who you are. I think I'm the only one who doesn't believe them," Quinn says. "You don't seem like that type of girl. You seem nice."

"Aww, thanks. You seem nice too Quinn," I say, acting all sweet even though inside, my blood is boiling. I can't believe Makayla. I never told anyone anything that she's done. She lied! She lied to me! I try not to stomp over to Crystal. I need to keep my cool, especially right now with Makayla right here.

"I can't believe Makayla!" I whisper. "She lied to everyone about me." I bury my head in my hands. I don't feel like doing art right now.

"Aww. You crying Olivia?" an all-too-familiar fake sweet voice says. "You a little baby? Do you need your binkey?" Makayla starts doing the evil laugh that annoys me so much. I'm already angry enough. That stupid laugh is the last thing I need right now.

That. Is. *It!* I have to shut up Makayla once and for all. I can't keep dealing with this. She lied. Nothing that's happened to me this year was my fault. It was all her. And I'm done. "You know what Makayla? I'm not crying. And you know what I found out this year? You *lied.* You lied about everything this year. I was here, thinking that this was my fault. But it's not. And I don't know why you hate me so much. I don't even know what I ever did to you! I've heard from many sources that you've been talking about me behind my back! Here I was, thinking you were a good friend. You weren't. You have been the worst friend to me." I don't sit down at first; that's a sign of weakness. I wait for her to comeback, but she has nothing. She just sits down in her seat. I'm actually in a state of shock. I won. I just won. She may never talk to me again, but I don't care. I don't need someone like her to talk to me again. Now, I know who my real friends are. They are NOT Makayla.

But I realize then that life as we know it has changed. I'm stronger than her now. All those times I wanted to say something but thinking about it made me too scared went behind me and I just feel strong. I still can't believe I won.

She's probably going to start talking about me again, but I don't care. I'm victorious today. And forever. Even if life as we know it has changed. Maybe it's for the better.

Chapter 4
The Beach

We're going on a field trip! We're going on a field trip! We're going on a field trip to the beach! I never thought we'd go on the field trip to the beach. We're not allowed to go in the water. But it's still a field trip.

Anyway, as the day approaches, everyone gets more and more excited. I am too, even though the only friend I have in that class is Jason. Science is the class we do everything in. I can't have any field trips in history or whatever, because that'd be too convenient for me. I don't really want to start talking to Jason because who knows what I might say if I'm not careful. I have to work really hard on my filter when I'm with him, considering how much I've embarrassed myself in the past. I've smiled like an idiot every time he's looked at me. Besides, he has other friends in that class. I don't think he'd want to spend all his time just talking to me, so I start trying to hang out with more people. If it isn't obvious, that doesn't work.

So, when the day of the field trip approaches, I go to the cafeteria with the rest of the science class. Luckily, Jason lets me sit near him. I blush as I sit down. It's really squishy on the bench, so I have to work really hard not to have any part of my arms touch him. I succeed, and I get lucky, because Mrs. Keddman says that we are going to be split up. I'm going to be on the bus and on the field trip with Tara. Crystal and Ella are together, but I don't care. They'll have fun. At least I'll have some time alone with Tara which is nice. We sit together on the bus.

Tara and I spend the entire 20 minute bus ride talking about everything from our favorite colors to the pizza in the cafeteria. When we finally get to the beach, I breathe in the air. It's salty and I think there is sand in the air from the wind. We walk out and they let us take our shoes off, so I feel the sand between my toes.

Mrs. Keddman says that we are going to a private place to explore and learn, so we all go up about a million stairs until we get to the top of the beach, then we have to climb down about a million stairs. I don't think anyone wants to do it. I don't think anyone wants to do anything other than go in the water. But we all do it anyway because we're at the beach and we should just be grateful for what we have right now. And, what we have right now is the ability to go on a field trip to the beach.

When we finally arrive, we sit down on the sand. It's really hot but we have to deal with it. About 10 minutes in, I decide that I should not have have been as excited about this. So far, all it's consisted of is sitting on the hot sand. Great. That's just *great.*

The rest of the day has some more activities that I like. We learn about a lot of different kinds of life on the beach and we actually do get to go in the water. It's really awesome. Bethany actually catches a horseshoe crab which is so cool. Tara and I find a lot of hermit crabs as we go, but we don't find anything even remotely interesting. Then again, Bethany has, like, 20/20 vision, so she can see everything that's on the ocean floor. I'm just lucky I didn't step on it. Ouch!

The field trip comes to a temporary stop at lunch time. We sit down on the sand and just eat and talk. The waves are getting really big. Maybe I can ask my family if we can come back here later tonight. When I tell Tara, she laughs. "Yeah right. My family would be like, 'You already went to the beach today Tara,' or something like that." I can't help laughing. She is amazing at impersonating her parents.

As the beach trip finally winds down, it's starting to get windy. I think it's almost 2:30 pm. We have to get a ride home from our parents when we get back to the school. Tara and I sit together again, but this time, we both listen to music on our phones. The bus stops in front of the school at 3:19 pm according to the clock on my phone.

George is with my mom and dad. He must have been picked up early. His school ends at 3:15 pm, so there is no way they'd already be here if he was picked up on time. I hop in the car. It's nice to be in the air conditioning after being in the hot sun all day. George keeps asking me random questions, but I just want to go home and be in my air conditioned room.

"Was the field trip good?" my little brother asks me.

Was it good? Yeah. Yeah, the field trip was very good. When I tell George he smiles contently and we pull into my house.

Chapter 5
Now that I'm used to it...

Now that it's just about the end of April, a lot of things are changing.

- I have to force the smile off my face when I see Jason, which is not a good thing because it means that *I CAN NO LONGER LOOK AT JASON!!!!!*
- I'm so close to being a teenager, but I'm not there yet. Which is stupid and awful because now I am jealous of Crystal, Tara, and Ella.
- I'm finally learning how to deal with the teachers...about a month before the end of the school year.
- I'm finally learning when to talk to Ella and when to talk to only Crystal and Tara.

So, I'm growing up. Which is great except for the Jason thing and the teenager thing. But, you can't win them all. Anyway, my goal for the end of this year is to learn how to talk to Jason without being better off having the words, "I like you Jason" tattooed across my forehead. My other goal is to somehow get Makayla to start being nicer to me, but I'm not sure I want to be friends with her after I found out she lied to me.

To be honest, I don't know why anyone still wants to be her friend. I have a feeling if she lied to everyone about me, she's lied to everyone about someone else too. Or maybe not. Because, I think I know what I have that she wants. Or should I say, "who" I have that she wants. It's a little someone named Ella Anderson.

It all makes perfect sense. Makayla sees me with Ella and gets jealous. But I'm going to keep my best friend. It's all going to be fine.

May

Chapter 1

The Presentation

The year is coming to an end now that it's May, and my teachers and all trying to jam as much knowledge into our brains before June 22nd. There are going to be new middle schoolers coming in, two of them being my brother and Crystal's sister.

That's why Crystal and I are in her car right now, 45 minutes before school's over, talking about how we want to present. We're doing a presentation for our little siblings. Fun, right? Since they're both in the same class, we thought we could talk to them about the middle school.

Except right now, a panic has come over me, and I'm doing everything in my power not to start freaking out. I'm only comfortable with what I am saying. Crystal and I have had no chance for practicing this. We don't really know what we're doing. We're winging it! I'm kind of nervous for what's coming.

I walk into George's classroom. He gives me a weird look. I nod and smile. I see Alexa staring at him, which makes me sick to my stomach. Alexa is 10, not a desperate teenage girl. I walk up to the front of the class with Crystal as Mrs. Greene, George's 4th grade teacher, introduces us. My stomach does a flip. I'm so excited but also extremely nervous. I mean, I'm not confident in what I'm saying. Wel went over her house a little while ago and we made a slide show. That's it. That's the only practice we've had and I don't really even know what I'm doing.

We stand in front of the class. Our slide show is behind us, the 9 and 10 year old boys and girls are staring at us, and Crystal and I give each other anxious glances. *This is it,* I think, my nervousness fading away quickly as I become more confident. *This is really going to happen. Something I've been planning for since April is finally about to happen.*

Crystal gives me a look that says start, and I say, "Hey guys! So my name is Olivia Hamilton and this is my best friend Crystal Jace. I'm George's sister and Crystal is Alexa's sister. So today we're going to talk to you about the big MS. MIDDLE SCHOOL!" I do crazy jazz hands and the class laughs. Crystal smiles too. I let out an internal sigh of relief. As of right now, they like me. I've just gotta keep it that way.

"The middle school is a fun and awesome place. The classes are longer and you have different teachers throughout the day," Crystal explains. Before I know it, it's my turn again, but it's easy to talk now.

"There are a lot of different UA's and you get to chose what most of them are. There's band, chorus, art, music, French, Spanish.." I trail off, counting off the points on my fingers. How am I able to talk to a group of 4th graders but not talk to to Jason who is a boy my age who seems to have no trouble talking to me? I turn to Crystal. "Am I forgetting anything Crystal?"

"I don't think so Liv."

I see George look confused but I give him a look that says that I'll answer him later. He rolls his eyes, and I'm almost positive that that means that I should just tell her that I don't want to be called Liv. But, Crystal is my best friend. If she really wants to call me Liv, she can.

The kids all liked me and when I ask them for questions, a few of them raise their hands. We take turns answering them. Before I know it, the presentation is over. I give the kids a lollipop and a pencil. Just like that, it's over. It was so much fun, but now it's over. I want to do it all again.

Chapter 2
Teen Book Battle

In our school, we have this thing called Teen Book Battle. Basically, it's this thing where you read at least 5 of the selected books and then you do games on them. The 5th and 6th graders have this thing called Rooster Games which is the same thing but with different books.

Anyway, my team is wearing tan. I'm mostly excited for a day of games instead of work but I'm also kind of like, "Who the heck owns tan clothing?" I'm kind of disgusted. I am a colorful person and I get *tan* as my team color? Why is tan even a team color?

But, I go out and buy a tan tee-shirt. It looks okay on me, but how good can tan look on a person? I have no friends in my group and it's turning out to be a disaster - a big huge disaster. I haven't even gotten to the worst part.

Here is my team for the book battle tomorrow:
- Makayla
- Eli
- James
- Theo
- Holly

AHHHHHHHHHHHHHHH! Why why why why why? Don't the kids know how much I hate these people? Well, not hate but strongly dislike? And, I think the feelings are pretty mutual! I have one simple request: Don't put me on a team with Makayla. What do they do? They put me with MAKAYLA!

School is possibly the worst thing ever. The worst! One of the things that adults do to get kids to go to school is offer to see their friends. I can't name one activity I've been put with my friends. But anyway....

On the day of the Teen Book Battle, I walk into school with my tan shirt. I have worn as brightly colored shorts as I can. I walk into the auditorium where we are supposed to meet and sit with my team. Next to Holly. At least she's a girl that is not Makayla. She ignores me. Big surprise. I sink down in my seat. I hate my team.

I enviously look over to Crystal and Ella who are on the same team. They both make friends so much easier than I do. It's stupid to be jealous of them but I am. I know, I'm my own person and all that stuff and I'm happy with who I am most of the time. When I'm not wishing I was someone who was athletic or more popular but not the mean type of popular, I love the person that I am. So, an even 6 out of 10. An even 3/5. That's more than half you know.

"Alright everyone! Welcome to the teen book battle. This is going to be a little different than the rooster games, so let's go over rules," the vice-principal starts. Good. These people will finally stop talking and I can finally stop feeling like a friendless dork. Of course I have no such luck?

Have I ever had such luck? No, the answer to my question is no. I suffer through the people who are talking while the teacher's talking (which of course is all of them) as I strain my ears to listen to the rules. If I don't know the rules, how do I know what my boundaries are? I could get in trouble. I try not to start hyperventilating.

Finally, the games begin. We all separate into our teams and I walk with (this is going to be a huge surprise) the team leader because she's the only one that tries to start a conversation. She's only one that seems to talk to me. Friendless dork? Check.

We enter into the classroom to begin the first game. Easy peasy. Our team wins that challenge, but it's mostly because of me. I read most of the books while these people seem to have read none. I decide to let them do the next ones.

Here's how that goes:

Activity 2

I try to let Holly do it, but she just keeps saying that I should do it and starts talking to Makayla. I didn't know Makayla had so many friends. I thought she was friendless because of how mean she is. What, is she the most popular girl in school now? I wouldn't be surprised if the answer to that question is yes.

Activity 3

Makayla tries to do it, which I have no problems with, but she still doesn't talk to me and I don't talk to her so we lose that challenge. I don't know why I let her do anything.

If we want to win, I should just try and take over the activities again. In a non-bossy, non-geeky sort of way. Which is probably impossible, so I decide not to do this.

Lunch. Finally lunch. I talk to nobody. I try to start of conversation. It doesn't really work out too well for me.

For the rest of the day, I try not to take over, but most of the time I end up doing so. The boys are not doing anything except talking about sports and I feel like I should be wearing a sign that says, "I'm not here to do your work." Do you know where I can get one of those? Or a place where I can make one with minimal trouble? Just kidding. But no seriously, do you know where I can buy one?

Chapter 3

The Sport I (thought) I wasn't Bad At

You know how I'm amazing at every sport? If you answered yes, go back and reread this entire book. Anyway, I finally found a sport that I'm good at. It's called field hockey. I'm not bad at it. Ella, Crystal, Natalie, Sierra, and I are all doing it too. I love having something I can do with my friends that I'm not bad at, especially when it's a sport. Crystal, Tara, and Lexi are all athletic and finally I won't be a girly-girl who likes rainbows and sparkles and colors and Disney Channel. (I'm still exactly like that.)

One of the best parts of field hockey is the fact that I have no Makayla. She's finally not interested in something that I'm doing. Finally! When Ella told me, it took everything I had not to let out an audible sigh of relief. Now, the coach is talking to us about field hockey.

We can't join the official team until high school. This is intramural. We all listen, holding our sticks and balls. Ella is bouncing beside me and Crystal is listening with wide eyes. I'm so excited. All my friends and I have wanted to do field hockey since 5th grade. Besides, my brother's doing soccer and basketball and baseball and football and lacrosse and he wants to do hockey, so I think I can do field hockey. Don't you?

The coach tells us to go on the field and practice our passes. "Great job Ella. Oh, Crystal, I like your hand formation. Sierra, you are looking great. Are you sure you haven't played before?" the coach praises everyone. Then, she gets to me. Me, holding the stick that same way as all my friends and hitting the stick the same way as all my friends.

"Olivia, hold your hands a little closer together and don't swing back before you hit the ball, okay?" she says. I nod. Great. The coach has been praising everything everyone does and she gets to me and this is her comment? My athletic ability has failed me once again. Then again, when has my athletic ability, or lack of athletic ability, not failed me?

Answer: Never.

I try not to let my face fall as I take her advice and pass the ball a little bit more. It's more accurate, but it disappoints me that I can't get it that way myself like my friends.

"Okay, now we are going to be working on our hits!" the coach yells out and everyone gets back into a straight line. Yes, finally something I can shine at. Yeah, I think you know me better than that. I can't shoot the ball for my life, but I think I can figure it out. It's field hockey. It's a sport played by girls. How hard can shooting the field hockey ball be?

I have must stop with this thinking that I have everything under control thing. I can't shoot the ball. I thought it would be easy to shoot the ball. You hit the ball with a little force with the stick and bam, goal is scored.

Let me just tell you now, it's not that easy. I don't think it will ever be that easy to score a goal in any sport. If there is a sport that it is easy to score or really do anything in, let me know. Please, let me know.

Anyway, as field hockey finally comes to an end, I run to my car with Crystal following behind me. We say goodbye to each other and I see Ella behind us. She's not talking to anybody and she takes a seat on the grass. I walk over to her and call my mom. I'm going to wait with Ella. Regardless of how she acts, Ella Caroline Anderson is my best friend. I never want that to change.

Chapter 4
The Tour to end all Tours

"Crystal!" I scream out. May's almost over and we both know what that means. It's time for the tour for the 4th graders that as SADD members get to lead. Crystal looks over at me and waves. We're coming in from the bus. I almost never see her in the morning. I guess it's luck since we're actually doing something fun today. I don't have to go to blocks 2-6. That's awesome, isn't it? I think it's awesome.

"Hi Olivia! Isn't this so cool? We're going to be showing the 4th graders around the school. And, we're just about done with May, so we're almost the oldest in the school." Crystal smiles at me and I continue walking into school with her. We keep talking about the school show around the entire time.

"Are you excited? Cause I'm excited!" I say with a huge smile.

"Uh, yeah I'm excited!" Crystal says. "I mean, hopefully Alexa won't be weird around George."

"I still don't know why she has a crush on George. He's my brother," I say, making a disgusted face. But in reality, I'm only half kidding. I mean, she can't help who she has a crush on. If it was up to me, for example, I'd have a crush on a much less popular guy than Jason. Maybe I'd like someone like Calub.

"Believe me, I've been asking her forever," Crystal says. I giggle and we open our lockers.

I walk to science. I like science for the most part now that I've gotten used to it. I sit down at my table. The kids are fooling around. Why am I the only girl in my group? I open up my book and start reading until announcements. I can't wait until the end of this block.

It doesn't come soon enough. I rush out of the classroom and meet Crystal at her locker with very minimal drama. We walk down the auditorium, smiling and talking the whole way. When we get down there, it's announced that the 4th graders will be arriving any second! Any second! How cool is that?

We all stand outside, holding the signs that will tell them where our groups are. I hold up our sign with a huge smile on my face and Crystal looks at me like I'm crazy. "Fine, you try holding the sign and looking inviting," I say, holding the sign out to her. She takes it and puts a fake smile on her face. I roll my eyes and grab it back, doing the huge smile I had before. Crystal smiles at me as the 4th graders get off the bus.

Most of the girls look around in wonder as the boys start fighting. I roll my eyes. When I was in 4th grade and I was doing the tour, I took it pretty seriously. I'm sad to see George fighting with his friend Alex. Oh no. My brother is not ruining my good reputation at this school. I yell his name and he runs over to my group.

"Hey! Olivia!" he says, annoyed. "I was playing with Alex."

"You weren't playing, you were fighting," I say matter-of-factly.

"Boys play differently than girls," George mumbles.

We lead the kids inside and go around the entire school. "Olivia? I have a question!" one girl shouts from the back. I nod in their direction. "When's lunch?"

"12:05 ," I answer. "You should be able to wait until then, right? I mean, if not, we can see if we can grab you something before, but the chances of that happening are pretty slim, I've gotta say." I stare at the girl. She is small with tan skin and brown hair. She has a sweet smile. I feel bad. She shakes her head as if to say, "I'm fine".

We walk some more. The kids find the gym fascinating, but I don't know why. For me, the gym is filled with a lot of bad memories, not something I'd find joyful much less fascinating.

After the gym, we take them to their hallway. They're going to talk with their teachers about the upcoming year, and we tour guides take a seat in the hallway. Luckily, Crystal engages me in some conversation. That's the good thing about having a friend like her. She can always make you feel better in your friendless moments.

Finally it's lunch. I am starving. I end up sitting with Crystal at a table with her sister. Alexa is mostly talking to her frien. Crystal and I are talking to each other.

"Can you believe the tours almost over?" Crystal asks me.

I shake my head. "I know. Something we've been looking forward to all year is actually over."

"Yeah, since 7th grade started. We were so young." She looks at me a little. "You've matured Olivia."

"Really?" I ask, blushing. Crystal nods.

"At the beginning of the year, you were way more random. You were funny at much different times, and you weren't popular."

"Gee thanks," I say.

"Relax Liv. I was only kidding about the popular thing," Crystal says. "And I meant it as a compliment. You're different now. And it's good different."

I look down. Sure, I know I've changed. I'm like 10 days away from being a teenager. But maybe Crystal's right. Maybe I've changed personality wise too. I did it. I became a whole new Olivia in 7th grade.

Chapter 5
Wow.

Wow. I can't believe I'm almost done with 7th grade. This month alone, I've grown up so much. Now, I'm 9 days away from becoming a teenager. I can't believe it. Plus, I got into High C! How amazing is that?

June

Chapter 1
My (gasp) 13th Birthday

I wake up on June 9th feeling completely different than June 8th. That's because after 13 years of waiting,

I'm finally a teenager. It feels good. I'm like whoa. Wow! I'm a teenager. After all this waiting, it's finally here and I couldn't be more excited. One of the best parts ever; it's on a Saturday this year! When I wake up, I blink twice as my eyes adjust to the light and see the sign I made the night before and stuck on my ceiling. Happy 13th Birthday, it reads. That's when I get the jump in my stomach and I just want to get up and run around. My dad and brother aren't here, George had a soccer tournament, and my mom is still sleeping, so I get dressed and go outside. Best day ever!

I have to be outside for a half hour before my mom comes in and asks me to take a shower. Done. I will do anything to make the party get here faster. Besides, after my shower, we get my cake and the decorations. So that's why, when I'm done, I get dressed in the same non-party clothes and eat cereal. It's not exactly my dream birthday breakfast, but it will do. Then, my mom and I head out.

We go to pick up the cake first. It's a donut cake shaped like a painter's pallette that says, "Happy 13th Birthday Olivia!" We have to wait in line for what feels like forever. How many donuts can these people want? My party starts at 2 pm and I know it has to be getting close. They should have a cake line and a "I'm going to take my time picking out my donuts" line. I should start that. I can't start that.

Finally, finally, *finally* we get my cake. I open up the box. It's awesome! I knew they could do a good job but I didn't realize they could do this! It's amazing! I shut the box and we walk out, ready to get the party decorations.

We arrive at the store a good 10 minutes later and I pick out every type of party decoration available: Streamers, tablecloth, confetti, a banner, etc..I have to limit it down to a few things, so I get to keep one package of everything I picked. This is going to be my 13th birthday party. The day I've waited for since forever is going to be done right.

When we get home, my mom takes a shower and I see that it's noon. I can't get dressed in my part clothes yet, so I write on the computer. Finally, 1:30 pm comes and I run upstairs and get dressed. I'm wearing a pink shirt with a coral, pink, purple and white skirt. It has little flower things on it. Then, I do my hair. It's naturally wavy, so I just brush it out and leave it. I look at myself in the mirror before I go downstairs. I look older. I feel older. I am older. I am thirteen.

My mom yells down that my grandparents are here. It's hard to hear over Peanut's barking. I run down the stairs and say hello to them. Then, I have to get the table and entire house for that matter set up. I start with decorations.

When the house looks absolutely perfect I sit down at my counter. More guests have started to arrive and I've said hi to all of them. Peanut has barked more today than in his entire almost 2 years of life. I just want to be done now.

I'm not however. I play upstairs in my bedroom with my cousins. It's hard. Some of them are 8 but another one is 14. I have to try to incorporate all of them. It doesn't work so well. Eventually, I just decide I'll play with each group one at a time.

When it's time for cake, as everyone is singing happy birthday, I realize this is one of the best days of my life. My entire family is here and I'll be having my friends over soon. I feel like I can do anything. I never want this feeling to change.

Chapter 2
George's Graduation and a Sleepover

Two more weeks are left of school. Two more weeks left of what has been the hardest year of my life. And for George, it's two weeks left of elementary school, which is really weird. When I went to middle school, he was going into 2nd grade. Now, he's leaving 4th grade with a bam.. called a graduation.

It's at 10:00 in the morning. I'm in the car leaving from school for his graduation. I'm in the backseat staring out the window. Crystal is sleeping over tonight but she wasn't in school. I think it's because she's going to school after the graduation, but I still don't know. She didn't tell me why she wasn't there. My big concern is that she's going to be sick and won't be able to sleepover.

When we finally get to George's elementary school, he's not outside yet. I see Natalie sitting in one of the chairs with her older sister, Erica, who is 14. She sees me and waves me over. I run over to her and sit in the chair next to her. "Hey Nat!"

"Hey Olivia!" she says. It's refreshing to be called Olivia after being called Liv for a while. We start talking for a little while, and I'm happy to see Crystal when she walks in with her family. I wave her over too and we start talking for a little while. She tells me she will be going to school after this, but I'm not. George is going to his friend's house. That means that I will have some time alone. Finally.

The graduation starts and I get up to start video taping. For my birthday, I got a camera and I've been dying to use it. The teachers start talking. They give a big speech and then they finally start saying all the kids names. Right there, between Hannah Fryer and Kole Hazard is George Hamilton. My brother is graduating and I have recorded all of it.

Satisfied, I sit back in my seat. Natalie has stood up and is watching her younger brothers, Lance and William, who are twins, as they graduate. I sit next to Crystal again and she watches Alexa. George is all upset as he walks out because he has to walk out with Hannah Fryer. He really doesn't want to walk out with a girl. At least after this he can stop complaining for a little while.

The graduation finally ends. I've had some time alone and at 4 o'clock, Crystal comes over. George is sleeping at his friend's house, which is nice. Crystal and I end up going to a movie, then we order a pizza. Well, no, that's not fair. My parents come with us to the movie and my dad orders the pizza for all of us, not just the two 13 year old girls.

At night, we are up in my room. She's on her air mattress and we're both in our pajamas. "That was really fun," she tells me. "Thanks for having me over."

I smile. "You're welcome. I'm not having a birthday party so..."

I also plan on doing something with Ella, but I haven't really done anything about it yet. Maybe she can come over sometime soon. I hope so.

At 11 o'clock, we decide to go to bed. I fall asleep after thinking about the entire day I've had. It wasn't that bad. I'm so excited that 7th grade is coming to an end. Not that I haven't had a good time this entire year, but you know, I haven't. Now I can finally finish it up right.

Chapter 3
You Have Gotta Be Kidding Me

We get our yearbooks on the day before the last day of school. I flip through it eagerly. I go to the 7th grade section of the yearbook. I go to the H section of the yearbook. Where am I? Where am I? I'm not in here. I'm not in the yearbook. No, that's crazy. I've gotta be in here somewhere.

I go the the student council section. No! Just because I'm not a vice president doesn't mean I'm not a senator! I mean, it's like they literally just cut me out of the picture with all the senators. I flip through to the SADD section. I'm there, in the group picture, you can see me in the back of it next to Crystal. I mean, it's a start. I flip through all the pages. I see a picture of Jason and his best friend Tim, a picture of Crystal during gym class, a picture of Ella and Makayla (oh come on), and a picture of Ava, Katie, and Lisa but no pictures of me. I groan inwardly. Was I just cut out? Or maybe Makayla was responsible somehow.

That's ridiculous and would never happen, I'm very aware of that. Makayla's never shown any interest in that sort of thing. But doesn't this seem like something that she'd do, especially if there is a picture of Ella and Makayla in the yearbook.

I bring the yearbook home and tell my parents about me, oh, I don't know, *not even being acknowledged in it.* Yeah, I'm not really in a good mood. At least tomorrow is the last day of school and I don't have to deal with Makayla until September. Yes! I run upstairs to my room and text Crystal.

Hey Crystal

Hey Liv! Crystal replies almost immediately. What's up?

Oh, nothing. Just that I'm not in the yearbook!

U have got 2 be kidding me! :-(

Nope.

Sorry Liv. Why would they leave you out of the yearbook?

I don't know. But I have a question.

Anything.

Would u be willing to do the yearbook with me next year? I'm going to ask the principal about it.

That would be so cool!

You really think so? You don't have to just say that you know.

No, I'm not just saying that. That would be super awesome. And I bet Tara, Katie, Ava, and Ella would do it too. It'll be fun. You definitely should ask Principal Williams about that.

So, then, I guess we've got a plan! My mom calls me down the stairs. Gotta go.

See you tomorrow Liv!

Last day of school! Finally! Okay, bye Crystal!

When I get down the stairs, I tell my mom my plan. She says it sounds like a good idea. Suddenly, not being in the yearbook doesn't seem so bad. I've got a plan.

Chapter 4
The Last Day of School

It's about 9 am on the last day of school and I can't believe it. I'm almost an 8th grader. How amazing is that?

Answer: Very amazing!

I'm going to start wrapping this book up now. I can't believe it! I'm almost done with school. Plus, I'm one year away from being the oldest in the school. I guess I've grown up more than I thought I did.

Crystal is right next to me as always and Ella is near Makayla. Makayla isn't talking to me. She hasn't since the incident with the diamond in the snow. I don't care. It's much better this way.

We're in history right now, and the teachers are just letting us sit where we want to sit. I'm near Crystal and we're watching KWN. I'm only paying half attention though, which isn't any different from the other times we've watched KWN. Am I supposed to pay full attention? I have no idea. It's the last day of school. What could they possibly do to me? I don't know how I'm supposed to pay attention to something like KWN at a time like this. How does anyone pay attention to this? I'm so close to the end of 7th grade I can't even believe it! Can you believe it? No. The answer is no.

As history class ends and the other classes begin, I get more and more excited. Finally, it's last block. Only one more hour until 7th grade is over. As excited as I am, I'm also kind of nervous. I mean, what happens after this? I don't know why, but I feel like this year went by way too quickly. I'm not sure how I'm supposed to feel.

I talk to Jason after it's over. "Hey, have a great summer Olivia," he says. He is smiling at me. I don't want to start freaking out or anything, but he is smiling at me. How amazing is that?

"You too. Um, yeah. I guess I'll see you in September, right?" I force out of my mouth. I'm really not concentrating on what I'm saying. I'm more trying not to smile like an idiot. Jason nods.

"Ready to go Liv?" Crystal asks. I nod.

"Bye Liv. Bye Crystal," Jason says, waving. I wave back.

"I think I'm doing better at talking to him," I say to Crystal when I'm pretty sure he's out of earshot. She laughs. I don't know if I should be offended. I mean, I know I'm bad at talking to Jason, but she doesn't have to disagree with me. But, yeah, I guess it's kind of fair. Hey, don't you start laughing at me too.

"Yeah right," she says. We laugh and I get on the bus. Maybe she can come over or sleep over or something soon. This is going to be the best summer ever. I'm going to be the oldest in the school next year. I get on the bus and become an 8th grader. After this whole year, I've made it.

Chapter 5
A Whole Year

The year is over. My book is over. This entire world is over because this book is over. And, 7th grade is over.

It started out with a huge eye-opener in September, where I learned that just because I'm not with

Ella doesn't mean we can't be best friends, and I learned that you sometimes can make new friends. You can make a lot of friends and keep them all. But if you're not careful, they can disappear, like in October, when I found out a shocking truth about Makayla. But maybe, just maybe, that was for the best. In November, I had my first crush. Now that I know what that's like, let me tell you, it's pretty hard to control what I say around him. But throughout the year, I got better at talking to him. In December, the fight between me and Ella got sparked by a single text. By January, we weren't really talking to each other anymore, but luckily, we made up in early February. In March there was Dalton Gommes, and after that, the year started to wind down. Now, the year is over and I'm getting ready to go into 8th grade. I can't wait to see where the summer takes me.

58126195R00080

Made in the USA
Lexington, KY
03 December 2016